RECKLESS HART

A CROSS CREEK SMALL TOWN NOVEL

KELLY COLLINS

BOOK NOOK PRESS

Cover design by Sly Fox

Edits by Show Me Edits

Edits by Melissa Martin

CHAPTER ONE

LAUREN

No good deed goes unpunished. Or at least that was my experience with the Lockharts. As I drove home, I thought about dinner with their family and concluded that Quinn Lockhart didn't care for me. During the "trial run" to prove I was qualified, I pointed out an unpaid debt he swore had been taken care of—he was wrong.

Moving up the front sidewalk to the little cottage I'd purchased, I considered this to be the strangest Sunday I'd experienced in a long time. As I pulled the keys from my purse, a sensation of being watched sent a shiver racing down my spine. I threw a cautious glance over my shoulder but saw nothing. I smoothed a hand over a prickling spot on my neck, hurried up the three concrete steps to the little wooden porch, and faced the charcoal-colored door. My mind still reeled from the frustrating but good-looking blond Lockhart brother.

I shook my head because all I could do was follow the numbers. I swear Quinn seemed ready to fight tooth and nail to prove I had no idea what I was talking about, but the data didn't lie.

His brothers seemed to think I'd make a great addition to the team, which led me to believe Quinn thought they could talk their old accountant into staying. Why else would he be against hiring me?

Ol' Brock was the CPA his dearly departed father hired and trusted. Clearly, Quinn didn't like change. Well, changes were coming if I had any say in things. I needed this job, and I wasn't letting one stubborn brother stand in my way.

I thanked my lucky stars they hadn't asked me for my letter of recommendation. I wasn't a liar, a cheat, or a thief, but I'd weasel my way into a good job if it meant feeding my daughter.

Sliding my key into the lock, I exhaled as it clicked slightly, and the deadbolt retracted. I pressed the door open and tiptoed into the silent living room. No light from the TV, no sound from the kitchen, no noise at all left me nervously touring the house. This was a new place where Fawn and I would start our lives over. Hopefully, every-thing would calm down and I'd be able to breathe.

Cross Creek was familiar to me because my grandparents, Norman and Ethel, had lived here all their lives and loved the little town. I spent many a weekend, and often weeks in the summer, visiting them. Back then, it seemed like the end of the earth. To a kid, it was boring, but to my adult self, the quiet respite would help me to regroup and reevaluate my life.

I opened Fawn's bedroom door, and my friend Missy put a finger to her lips as she cradled my four-year-old daughter. With a smile, I motioned for her to join me in the living room. Missy had been my best friend for as long as I could remember, and when she found out I was moving to Cross Creek, she packed up her life and moved to nearby Silver Springs to be closer.

She untangled herself from Fawn's sweaty embrace and stood, testing the floor as if not trusting the hardwood not to squeak. Then, like a villain from a cartoon, she tiptoed in my direction, hands in front, dangling like T-Rex arms, her knees almost coming to her chest with each step.

Her messy black curls and bright blue eyes were stunning but warm and reminded me of my mother who was kind to a fault. I smiled at her playful expression. We crept out of the room like teenagers sneaking out of the house for a party featuring alcohol and boys.

"How did it go?" Missy slung an arm around my shoulders and squeezed me as we headed into the kitchen.

She shook her head as she took in the budget furniture I'd bought to fill the place. As she ran a fingertip along the ugly, cheap Formica table, I tried not to remember the beautiful things my previous home had.

I didn't think about my prior life unless I had to.

Letting out a sigh, I grabbed a bottle of wine from the housewarming basket my mother sent along. Missy pulled the bottle opener out of the drawer.

I smiled, wondering how the heck she knew the thing would be there.

As if reading my expression, she scanned the tiny kitchen. "I mean, it's the most logical place." She shrugged. "It's within reach of the fridge and the glasses." She demonstrated by touching both. "This place would turn me into an alcoholic quickly."

I laughed, looking at the dingy kitchen. The place could use some updating and a heavy-handed deep cleaning, but I didn't hate it. "I know it's not pretty, but I like it." I inhaled deeply. "It smells like home and freedom. You know, a fresh start."

She took the wine bottle from me and opened it. Her eyebrows shot up to her forehead and disappeared under her bangs. "That smell is black mold."

I laughed. A *clickity-clacking* noise drew my attention toward the door. "Lucky!" My daughter's little one-eyed, snaggle-toothed, wire-haired terrier came trotting up to me, his tongue hanging out of his mouth to the right. It was so long, I worried—as I always did—that he might trip over the darned thing.

I crouched down to pet him, and he did a little dance with his front feet before lifting one leg and curling the pad of his paw back. Fawn picked this winner out at the pound after hearing ugly dogs rarely found loving homes. She'd shown him every bit of love a dog could hope for. The two were partners in crime and damned near inseparable.

Missy offered me a glass of wine, and I stood up, took it from her, and made my way to the table. Sitting in one of the rickety chairs, I sipped the sweet red. "I think I'll be happy here." I stared at the wine in my glass and rotated it by the stem. "It's a good place. Even Lucky thinks so." As if understanding me, he moved toward me and flopped under my chair. Within seconds, the small dog was snoring so loudly, you'd think a bear had found its way into my kitchen.

"I hope so because you deserve to be happy." She smiled, raising her glass, which held only a splash of wine.

"You could leave your car and take an Uber home then stay and have a full glass." She was the type of person who didn't like to drive even after a single sip of wine—a trait I respected.

She shook her head. "I promised my mom I'd take her to her class tomorrow. You know her, she's not ready to trust any driving services."

I giggled. Missy's mom didn't trust anyone, let alone a stranger who took her places for money. Every time a ride service was mentioned, she'd go off on a tangent about people willingly getting into rapists' or murderers' cars. Still, her mother was fun and sweet, even if she was opinionated.

"Are you going to be okay?" Her stare weighed me down, and I knew she'd see right through a lie, so I told her the truth.

"I think so." I didn't have a more concrete answer than that. Not yet. I had Fawn, a roof over my head, a job prospect, and a fresh start. Barring any disasters, I'd be okay. Lucky let out an ungodly snort that shook him awake. He glared at Missy as if she'd woken him, then promptly went back to sleep.

"And this job, do you think it's a sure thing?"

I didn't know the answer to that. Quinn seemed determined not to hire me. Lifting my shoulders, I stared forward, not focusing on anything.

"That response lacked confidence." Missy's tone had me flashing a false smile because I didn't want her to worry. I did enough of that for both of us.

"Oh, I've got the job." Over Quinn's dead body, I'd bet. No doubt he'd spend the whole night trying to explain to his brothers why I wasn't a good fit, and how hiring me would ruin everything they'd worked hard and long for.

I downed the rest of my wine and set the empty glass on the table.

"Okay then. Hug me. I have to get home." Missy set her untouched glass on the counter before flinging her arms wide. I stood up and hugged her, noticing that she squeezed me extra hard before letting go. Her gaze met mine. "You've got this. You're amazing at what you do, and those guys would be fools not to hire you. And if they're all hot..." She winked.

"Hot and married." Or dating, at least. Except for Quinn. Of course, the one guy who seemed to hate my guts would be sinfully attractive and the only available Lockhart. "Besides, I'm not looking for love. I've given up men, remember? If the convent allowed mothers with children, I'd be tucked inside a nunnery."

Missy knew me well enough to know if I said something, I meant it. And I was swearing off guys for the foreseeable future. I didn't want to get hurt again, and the only way I could ensure that wouldn't happen was to keep men at a distance.

"Ugh. You're too young and hot to be single. Besides, black isn't your color." She headed to leave, and I stayed in hot pursuit.

"Black is everyone's color." She opened the front door. "Maybe I should date you."

With a grin on her face, she turned to look at me. "Not really my type." She planted a hand on her hip, then quickly pulled me in for another hug. "It's flipping cold out here! Warm me before I run out and turn the heater on." A moment later, she raced down the walkway toward her car, her breath silver in the air as darkness drowned out the last bit of light.

The engine roared to life, and I heard her through the window telling the car to hurry the frick up and get warm.

With a chuckle, I locked up but noticed Lucky eyeballing me. "Need to go out?" I waited for him to either trot to the door or walk away.

He stared for a few seconds, then walked toward Fawn's room, no doubt ready to climb in her warm bed and hide under the covers. I smiled at the overload of cuteness that thought brought me before I padded back into the kitchen. Pouring myself another glass of wine, I tried to stifle the unease settling inside.

The letter of recommendation in my bag seemed to mock me from the other room. I gulped down my wine in an unladylike fashion and sighed.

What would happen if I had to give it to them? Would Quinn see right through me and know I forged the letter? I hadn't quit my previous Fortune 500 company on good terms, as I claimed in the letter. Nope, I'd been fired. It wasn't my fault. Well ... not really my fault.

As for the Lockharts, I'd done what I thought I had to do to secure the job. What else could I do?

Pouring a half glass, I stared at a spot on the shabby laminate flooring and brought both arms close to my chest as if that would simulate the hug I desperately needed.

Someone knocked on the door, and when I jumped, my wine sloshed dangerously near the rim. There was a pause before whoever was on my front porch knocked again. It was a hard knock, like that of a cop ready to bust in and make an arrest. My only crime was loving the wrong people.

I ignored the continued rapping. The only person I'd expected had already visited. Whoever was here, I didn't invite them, and they weren't welcome.

CHAPTER TWO

QUINN

"I still think she's a good fit." Noah smiled as Kandra patted his shoulder. The video conference call reminded me too much of last Sunday's dinner that Lauren sat in on to prove she could get along with our family.

While it was Sunday again, there was no family dinner tonight because Mom had a slight cold and didn't want to risk getting anyone sick. Angie also mentioned not feeling well, so we'd opted for a conference call instead of an in-person meeting. I still didn't understand my brother's logic—who cared if they liked her. If we hired her, it was to do a job, not be our friend.

I stared at them, then scanned the screen as my brothers and their significant others smiled and nodded in agreement. Did they not see what I saw? Everything was too good to be true. The blonde *oozed* trouble. "Oh, well, if Noah says she's a good fit, then let's hire her," I said with a dose of sarcasm. "But I've got questions." Noah didn't do the hiring, *I* did, and I'd learned that people will say and do anything to get what they want.

Noah lifted both shoulders. My brother's stares felt like sharp icicles digging under my skin. I glared directly at Noah. He was stepping on my toes, and I'd take him out back and beat his ass if I had to, like we did when we were younger.

"Quinn, don't you think you're acting like a child?" My mother's soft tone didn't take the sting out of her words. "She seems like a wonderful young woman."

Her statement told me why my brothers had asked her to sit in on this call, and I didn't appreciate their manipulation of the situation, pitting Mom against me.

Besides, I disagreed. Something about Lauren didn't sit right. Why had she moved out of the big city to our little town? Why did she have ghosts in her eyes? Why did she seem nervous—no, *terrified* —when I asked for her credentials, years of experience, and letters of recommendation? What was she hiding?

Noah's gaze slid toward another panel in the conference call. Then he lowered his head and stared down, refusing to look at me.

"I think we're done talking about the matter. At least until you've had some time to cool down," Mom said as she smiled at me. I wished we were sitting at the dinner table so I could kick Noah's shins with my steel-toed boots. That would teach him not to pull bullshit like this.

"You're looking lovely, Angie." Mom smiled at Ethan and Angie, quickly changing the subject, and I hunched my shoulders. I knew her angle before she spoke again. "Quinn, there's someone out there waiting for you."

I lifted a hand. "Don't even. Love has made you all soft, and I'm not interested. You know … once bitten, twice shy." Maybe I'd been interested in someone at one point, but that was years ago. Besides, loving someone was reckless, and I wasn't about to let that happen again.

"Quinn, don't you think you should open your heart again? That was fifteen years ago. It's time to let her go." Mom's voice and words offered support and warmth. She was wrong, though. Some things you couldn't let go of, forget, or forgive.

Tension rose as silence prevailed.

"Don't you think you went hard on Lauren at dinner? You were rude, man." Bayden eyed me, and Miranda elbowed him. As the sheriff and the love of my brother's life, she got away with stuff like that.

"She's not right for the job." I couldn't understand how they didn't have that same gut feeling that she'd screw everything up. Since they had fallen in love, all of their intuition seemed to go out the window. I took a sip of my beer and stared at Bayden, daring him to keep talking.

"She seems like a solid choice. Is there maybe another reason you're against hiring her?" Noah crossed his arms and leaned back in his chair while studying me.

"Maybe you're afraid you'll fall for the beautiful blonde?" Ethan's casual question didn't help matters, and I resisted the urge to drive to his house and teach him to mind his own business.

"How would you feel if I came to dinner and blindsided you? You're taking over my job. This has nothing to do with the fact that she's an attractive woman." I glanced at Ethan. "Imagine if I suddenly started designing projects. Or if I did whatever the hell it is you do, Noah." I scowled at my brother, knowing full well what his job entailed, but I wanted him to feel as insulted as I had. "Let me walk in and take over everything. You guys put me in this position because I'm good at reading people, and you know I'll hire the best."

Heads lowered, and my mother blinked, silent for this part of the conversation.

There was an underlying issue here. I was the only Lockhart brother not taken. "I know you're trying to set me up. You think I'll fall for this girl, and I won't be the pathetic, lonesome brother you all have to feel sorry for. Well, stop feeling bad for me. I'm living the life I want." I closed the laptop, effectively ending the call and resisting the urge to chuck the computer across the room. Just because my life didn't look like theirs didn't mean I wasn't happy. I was able to go out, have fun, and do whatever I wanted without asking for permission. That was more than I could say for my brothers.

Love was for fools and idiots, and I was neither. A long time ago, I swore never to let someone close again, and I'd kept my promise. Jumping headfirst into love was how you wound up hurt. I was completely happy with casual.

I picked up my phone to sort through the applications I'd saved. Or better yet, maybe I could talk Brock into staying. The guy had signed on with Dad way back when the company started and seeing him go felt like losing a part of the family. I'd miss him because I knew things wouldn't run as well without him.

And to think, Lauren had tried to drag his name through the mud, claiming some discrepancy. Brock didn't make those kinds of mistakes.

My phone rang, but I ignored the call because I knew it was Noah and I'd heard enough already.

All my brothers sure had changed since they'd all found love. They were arrogant know-it-alls, and they were driving me nuts. What would Dad say if he were here to see them hire some woman so they could play matchmaker? What would he think about them dismantling his company by letting Brock walk away and bringing in someone we know nothing about? Noah wouldn't have checked her credentials; he was out of his element trying to hire someone. He probably didn't know how or what to check to make sure she was even qualified.

She could've been some girl who was chasing big money and found herself in over her head. I'd dealt with enough guys doing the same crap not to be fooled by Lauren.

I sorted through the applications and put them into folders: no, maybe, and yes. The application questions I'd written gave me insight. The way people described themselves, how they presented their answers, and the words they used said a lot about them. Everything in the application gave away traits and personality types that influenced who fit into what folder.

The young man who mentioned a fresh new take on a tired profession went into the no pile. Some things didn't need updating, and accounting was one of them. I needed someone professional and articulate, with an ounce of intelligence. I wasn't looking for Einstein, but they had to know how to do the job right.

I came across Lauren's application and stared at the document without opening it before moving it to the maybe folder. I didn't want to hire her because I didn't trust her. Yeah, maybe I was skeptical based on my prior experiences, but there was also something off about her responses to basic questions. So, I'd go through every other application on file first, and if I didn't find a perfect match for the company, then I'd consider looking in her direction.

My phone rang again, and I glanced at the screen. It was Mom this time, and I didn't dare ignore her call.

"Hi, Ma." I shoved my laptop away and sat back on my couch, mentally preparing for the scolding that was coming.

"Don't punish Lauren because of Ashley."

Her words made my throat burn, and I swallowed hard.

"Ashley is never coming back, baby. She's married, has kids, and loves her husband. I really wish you could move on." Despite her loving tone, my go-to response was anger.

"That's not what this is about." The ache in my throat almost choked off my ability to speak. "Dad taught us better. We don't hire people because they're potential dates. He'd be furious if he knew what they were doing." Didn't she see what a dangerous game this was?

"Don't sell her short. Noah wouldn't have picked her because she's beautiful or a potential match for you, Quinn. She's a smart woman." Her words and tone made me wonder if they were all plotting to set me up.

"Whose side are you on, Mom?"

She laughed. "Oh, my headstrong boy, I'm on all sides."

That was where the problem lay for me. She didn't get it. "I'm not on any side but the company's side. I won't let Dad's legacy be reduced to dirt because Noah hired someone to get me a date. It's wrong." Where was the integrity? Dad and Mom raised us better than that.

"Quinn, you're still looking at things wrong. He's not trying to hire her for you. She would be an excellent addition to the company." Mom sounded hopeful, as if she could talk me into seeing how great of an idea this terrible plan was. "Her being your type is a bonus and a coincidence."

"Right, and today the sky was purple."

"Actually, it kind of was." Mom went silent for a moment. "Not everyone looks through the same lens. All Noah is seeing is a woman who's looking for a job and has the skills we need. We're not trying to fit a square peg in a round hole."

There it was; blind trust. "Noah doesn't know what goes into hiring. An unintentional mistake is still a mistake that could cost us. We can't mess around with accounting. An error on her part could wind up shutting us down for good or leaving us with the IRS on our tails. It's not worth the risk."

"You think Noah's trying to hire her on a gut feeling having done no research? Does that sound like your brother?" She was chastising me. "If anyone is having a gut reaction, it's you. Don't hold yourself to a different standard. Go with the facts and not the feelings."

There was no getting through to her. "I have a lot of work to do, Ma. I have to go. I love you."

We said our goodbyes and hung up. I stared at my screen with those three yellow folders that said no, maybe, and yes. As I sifted through the applications again, I realized I was stupid. I knew how Noah's mind worked, and while I didn't think he'd hire her outright, I knew he'd say no to everyone else I chose.

I clicked on the maybe folder, scrolled down, and opened Lauren's file.

My aversion to hiring her wasn't personal. She seemed like a nice enough woman, but dammit, my gut twisted when I was near her, and that had to be a sign. Lauren was trouble.

CHAPTER THREE

LAUREN

Monday, I hung out with Fawn, waiting to hear from the Lockhart brothers. Two weeks after the dinner with the family and I was losing hope. Fawn and I had finger-painted, explored our yard, and discovered a tree she wanted to climb. I took pictures to send to Mom, Dad, and Missy, but despite the fun of the day, the pressure drove me mad.

When evening rolled around and darkness fell, the stress of unemployment weighed heavily on me. Bills were waiting to be paid, and my meager savings were dwindling. While I could lean on my parents for help, I didn't want to have to. It was important to me to do this on my own and prove to myself I could.

"Fawn," I called. "Bath time." Perched on the edge of the tub, I ran the water as she squealed and raced through the house. Her chubby little feet slapped the hardwood as Lucky's nails clacked right behind her.

By the time she made it to the bathroom, she was down to socks. I smiled, knowing full well there'd be a trail of clothing throughout the house.

Without hesitation, she hurried and threw a leg over the edge of the tub, dipping her sock-covered foot in the water. The thought of wet socks made me cringe, and I tried to stop her. "Honey, no socks in the bath."

She leveled a stare at me. "Yes, socks." Pointing at her feet, she assured me she was wearing socks, and I held back a laugh.

"How will we get your feet clean?"

She shrugged, instantly going for her bath crayons, and selecting her favorite color—yellow. As she drew on the tiled wall, I watched Lucky creep closer. He put both paws up on the edge of the tub to watch her bathe. With all his fierce protectiveness, this little terrier didn't know he was no bigger than a lunch box.

"What are you protecting her from?" His ear twitched, but otherwise, he ignored me. Fawn sang in her high-pitched voice while I reached for her soap.

Lucky leaned in, and I let him sniff the container before using it. This was the ritual—a ritual the little dog started the moment she picked him out.

"What do you want for your birthday?" I asked, thinking about the upcoming date. I had months left to plan, but I wanted to see what she hoped for.

"Colors." She smiled at me as I worked shampoo through her short blonde curls. Her big blue eyes met mine before she went back to scribbling yellow on the wall, as if she could paint everything in her favorite color.

"Just colors? Nothing else?" I'd figure out other things to introduce her to, but my girl loved her art. She shook her head, still intent as I lathered her short locks. "How old are you going to be this year?" I asked.

Lucky licked at the bathwater. Shooing him away, I listened to her answer.

"I don't know, maybe sixteen?"

I couldn't hold back a chuckle — she was my silly little girl, the light of my life. I could get through anything as long as I had her.

She continued to play while I washed away the soap.

With a towel in my hand, I said. "It's getting chilly. Time to get out."

She stood and stepped out with a huge, open-mouth grin on her face as she let me wrap her up and hold her close.

"I love you, Mommy," she whispered.

"I love you too." I rested my chin on her head, staring at the little dog who took it upon himself to dry her ankles with his tongue. She giggled, and I finished drying her before pulling her into my lap to strip off her soaking wet socks.

Ten minutes later, she was dressed in her nightgown and tucked into bed. I read her favorite story about unicorns finding their way home. She curled against me, her little hand gripping my thumb as she drifted off to sleep. "Maybe sixteen," I whispered, a smile on my face as I smoothed her damp curls and remembered her silliness.

A knock startled me and sent Lucky into a barking frenzy. I quieted him, slipped from Fawn's bedroom, and rushed to the door.

The person on the porch kept banging, and Lucky followed, letting out a low, menacing growl as if he were a dog ten times his size.

I yanked it open, and my heart seized as I looked at my ex.

"Mike, what are you doing here?" I could hardly breathe because my mouth dried up like I was storing sand and it was sifting down my throat.

His russet red-brown hair and bright blue eyes made him as handsome as ever, but I knew better than to be drawn in by his good looks. He was like a poisonous flower The beauty drew in the prey, but total destruction was all that awaited. Behind the good looks was everything that could take you down and make sure you never got up again.

Lucky barked like a rabid dog. I hushed him, but he wouldn't listen. Instead, he dashed into the yard and came back at Mike like he needed running room to get momentum.

Mike sidestepped the attack, turned to me, and ran a hand through his hair. He flashed that sexy smile that melted my heart years ago. "You won't believe this, but the water main at my place broke. It flooded the house and street."

"I'm sorry to hear that." I crossed my arms, careful to block the doorway as I sized him up. "That's a long way to drive to tell me your story. Is your landlord putting you up?" If staying here was why he wound up on my doorstep, it wasn't happening. "Lucky!" I called the little cyclops as he ran back and forth and bolted past Mike to stand at my feet.

"Unfortunately, no." Mike seemed to search my expression, as if looking for a crack to weasel his way in. "He's not obligated since it wasn't a line break in the house, and he's not legally required to pay for a place for me to stay."

He stepped closer, but I held my ground, unwilling to let him push his way inside. He stopped short with that smile still on me as Lucky's growl grew more menacing. "Oh, come on now. You won't make your husband sleep in his car, will you?"

"Ex-husband." I ground the words through clenched teeth. "And don't talk about yourself in the third person, it's weird."

He chuckled. "You're still funny ... and beautiful." He reached out to touch my hair, his fingertips gentle as he dragged his knuckles down my cheek. "I miss you, Lauren, and I miss Fawn. When I needed a place to stay, I thought of home and you two."

"You can't be here." I tightened my crossed arms as if that would be enough to keep him from ripping out my heart and stomping on it. "Go stay with your girlfriend."

"I can't. She's mad at me. Please say yes?" He shot me that disarming smile again, but I knew I couldn't, shouldn't, wouldn't let him back in.

"I'm sorry, but I can't let you back into my life." I stepped back and attempted to close the door, but he spoke again.

"What would your parents say? And what would Fawn think,

when she gets older, if she knew you turned me away when I needed you the most?"

My parents would tell me to listen to my gut, but Fawn might hate me for leaving him out in the cold.

With a sigh, I bent down and picked up Lucky. "I'm sorry, little guy." I opened the door wider for Mike, walked down the hallway, and took Lucky to the garage. "I hate this as much as you do."

I brought him into the dark, barren space and grabbed the padded dog bed from the shelf, placing it under a heavy-duty storage rack. Grabbing his blankets, I covered him as he crawled into the bed, head down, tail low, and with a defeated hunch to his back.

"I love you. It's just one night. I'm sorry." My heart broke for the little terrier, but I knew better than to leave him in the house. Without me or Fawn present, Lucky would tear into Mike. After the last time the dog bit him, he swore if it happened again, he'd file charges to have Lucky put down. The only reason Lucky had been spared was I had proved he didn't have a mean bone in his body toward Fawn or myself. My parents vouched that he was a friendly dog, but it was Fawn's tears that saved the terrier.

Planting a kiss on his head, I covered him up and went back inside. Mike wandered through the living room, stopping to grin like a kid who'd gotten his way. "I would never have imagined you in a place like this. I'm proud of you."

I crossed my arms, my guard up again. I didn't care if he was proud of me. "Be gone before Fawn wakes up in the morning."

His expression fell, the change slight enough that I almost missed it before his smile returned.

"She wakes up at seven, so set the alarm on your phone." I didn't want to be in the same room as him, and I didn't want to have to wake him up and show him out in the morning.

I waited, feeling prickly as seconds ticked by, while he said nothing. Finally, he threw his arms wide, looking as happy as a kid in a candy store. "Of course! I'm grateful not to sleep in the cold. My car isn't comfortable."

"I doubt my couch will be." I walked down the hallway and opened the linen closet to get sheets and blankets. When I closed the door, I jumped back, not expecting him to be on the other side.

"It's fine. Thank you." He took the sheets and blankets from me, his hands brushing mine as he pulled them from my grasp. His gaze locked on me with an intense energy that left me shifting nervously and looking away.

"You're welcome. Don't forget to set the alarm." With that, I left the room. At the last minute, I turned away from my bedroom door and made my way into Fawn's room to curl up with her.

My phone chimed in my pocket, and I rolled my eyes, wondering what Mike wanted now.

Pulling it out and turning the volume off, my heart leaped as I noticed the text wasn't from my ex-husband but from Noah Lockhart.

I sat up, opening the message with trembling fingers.

Hello Lauren,

I apologize for the informality of sending our decision through a text. We're a small family company, so our methods may be unconventional. I wanted you to know you've been hired. Congratulations and welcome to Lockhart Construction. Please send your hiring paperwork to Quinn. We're excited to have you on the team. Let me know if you accept or not so we can move on to the next candidate. Thank you and talk to you soon.

Noah Lockhart

A phone number followed, which was no doubt Quinn's.

I got the job. I jumped out of Fawn's bed, doing a silent dance, and trying to hold back a victory screech.

Mike always told me that my emotions were immature and my refusal to cage my joy bothered him, but I wasn't married to him anymore, and I'd do a happy dance if I wanted to.

Life was looking up.

I'd gotten the job, but I still had to send my information to Quinn, and that included my letter of recommendation.

That thought sobered me, and I lowered onto Fawn's bed, wondering what would happen next. Not being completely transparent to the Lockharts didn't feel right—they seemed like good people. Still, I had a daughter to feed, and I'd do whatever it took to protect her.

CHAPTER FOUR

QUINN

"Be mad at me, little brother, but I already hired her last night." Noah's words made me angry, and I was tempted to hang up on him. "I think she's the best candidate for the job."

I couldn't believe he would be so impulsive and not even discuss it with me. He was acting like the old me, not caring what anyone else said and just doing what I wanted.

"Does Kandra know you have a thing for this chick?" Jokes. I could still make jokes at my brother's expense, though what I wanted to do was kick him in the shins and run. What was the point of me working for the company if I didn't have a say in the part that was my responsibility?

I rubbed the toe of my sock over an imperfection in the honey-colored hardwood floor. There was no bump, just an odd knot in the wood's grain that always compelled me to touch it. One day I'd likely wear a hole in the floor in that spot.

Noah's laugh grated on my nerves. "I think you're the one that's hot for her, and that's why you don't want to hire her because you're afraid you might actually fall for her."

"Not a concern. She's not my type."

"She is so your type. She's like—"

"Don't go there."

"Fine, but if you want to know the truth, Lauren is prettier than Ash—"

I covered my ears. Why did my brothers think I needed love to be happy? I was perfectly content on my own and not susceptible to womanly wiles like the rest of them.

"Then why are you against hiring her?" Noah seemed to hold his breath.

"Because you and Kandra are sweet together. I'd hate for this woman to ruin all of that since you've got a thing for her."

Noah held up his hand. "Okay, stop. Now isn't the time for your jokes. Lauren is capable of filling the position. Why do you refuse to acknowledge that?" Noah's annoyance appeared in his clipped tone, but it wasn't enough to make me want to back off.

"Why do you refuse to acknowledge that, by hiring her, you're stepping on my toes? You keep telling me how great she is, but where are the facts to back up that claim?" I sat down on my leather recliner and lifted the footrest.

Noah sighed. "I looked at her resume, and to be honest, I think she's overqualified for the job."

I'd looked at her resume too, and she was definitely overqualified, which was a red flag for me. "And that doesn't strike you as odd? She worked for a Fortune 500 company before us, and suddenly she moves from the big city to Cross Creek to keep books for our construction company. It makes little sense."

"Don't forget she's Ethel and Norman's granddaughter." Noah's point only poked a hole in my discomfort.

"We aren't a linear move for her, Noah. This is a step down—a big step." My brother wasn't this dense. There was no way we could compete with her previous salary or benefits. None of this made a lick of sense, and he knew it.

"Maybe she was tired of the city and wanted a slower lifestyle. Some people aren't happy in high-powered jobs long term."

"We can't run our business on maybe."

"You know what you could do, Quinn," he said in that matter-of-fact, big brother tone that had me scrunching my face and mocking him silently. "You could ask her these questions since her life story is that important to you. I doubt any of that has any bearing on if she can do the job, though."

Before I could figure out another joke to make at his expense, he spoke again.

"Look, I have to get off the phone. Talk to Lauren, and..." he sighed, "just give her a chance, okay? And unless you have a good reason, she's staying."

He hung up, and I stared at my phone. I couldn't believe he hired her without getting the green light from me. Why was I so against her? I had a list that started with a gut feeling and ended with the point that the choice should have been mine. Even in my own mind that sounded suspect.

My phone dinged, and a message popped up from an unknown number.

Hi, this is Lauren. Here's the information Noah requested. Thanks for the opportunity. I look forward to working with you.

Lauren

Informal text. What a nightmare. I opened the information packet and saw everything I'd been asking for the entire time. It was all there from her expanded application, letter of recommendation, and heck, she'd sent a copy of her transcripts. Refusing to be impressed by my casual glance at the information provided, I looked at her address.

Yep, I was going to show up unannounced and uninvited and try to figure out where the strange feeling she gave me came from. Yes, I felt something for her, but it resembled indigestion. Something about her dug at me, but I couldn't put my finger on it. I was a *go by my gut* guy, and it said it was time to figure things out.

I pulled on my boots and looked at myself in the mirror, hoping my dark jeans and blue button-down wouldn't be too informal for this impromptu interview of sorts. This was my part of the business, and I had the final say.

The drive to her place was a blur of thoughts. What would I say? What questions should I ask?

I pulled into her driveway and parked, noticing a man staring into her front window. Hopping out of my truck, I walked up to him, making sure I read the situation right. "Everything okay?" I asked, hearing a little dog losing its mind somewhere inside the house.

He jumped, turning to glare at me. From his pinched expression, it was like he considered me something he tracked in on his shoe.

He stood upright and walked toward me with a smarmy smile on his face. "I'm Mike, Lauren's husband. And you are?" He thrust his hand toward me.

I refused his handshake, uneasy about the whole situation. What husband lurked outside like a peeping Tom?

Was Lauren married? She'd said nothing about her marital status at dinner with his family. She'd painted herself as a single woman, close to her parents, and leading a quiet life—or planning to, now that she'd moved away from the bustle of the city.

He lowered his hand, and his stare intensified as his smile faded. "I didn't get your name."

"I didn't give it." I glanced at the front door, wondering if I needed to call Miranda. "Is Lauren home?" Mostly, I wanted to check in with Lauren to make sure calling the sheriff wouldn't upset her life if the guy was, in fact, her husband. I didn't trust him one iota.

He chuckled. "I like you, my man."

I didn't care if he liked me or not. My gut told me the guy was a clown. The little dog continued to yap away, and I grew more concerned and walked up the steps to ring the doorbell.

"Lucky, no." I could hear Lauren's voice on the other side of the door, and the dog went silent. "Be a good boy, okay? I don't want to have to put you back in the garage."

She opened the door, looking beautiful in a gray tank top and black yoga pants—the kind designed to drive men mad. I was determined not to notice, but while I wouldn't admit it to my family, I found Lauren attractive.

The dog leaped at my feet. My body tensed, but he raced past me to bark at the other guy, who squared off like a kicker about to punt the ball.

"Mike, don't!" Lauren rushed past without looking at me and gathered up the mutt as I struggled to process the wall of information slamming into me. She gripped the dog to her chest as she glared at the guy. "Why are you here?" Something seemed to register, and she snapped her attention to me. "For that matter, why are *you* here?" Confusion exploded behind her eyes, and she clung to the little dog as if protecting him ... or hoping he could save her.

I never liked small dogs, but the thought of this guy kicking it bothered me. I mean, how much damage could the little ankle-biter do? With his tongue hanging out as it did, he didn't appear to have a tooth left in his head. Was the guy afraid of getting gummed to death?

If he was her husband, why did the animal want to take a bite out of him? The humor of the little one-eyed, no-toothed, tongue-hanging-out dog named Lucky almost pulled a smile out of me, but I resisted.

"I just got here, and your husband was looking in your windows—"

"Ex-husband." She glared at Mike, who shook his head slightly as if disagreeing.

"Do you need me to call Miranda? She's the sheriff and my

sister-in-law." The man stiffened and he didn't appear to breathe while he stared at Lauren.

She glared right back as if she hadn't heard me, then glanced toward the house and gave her head a slight shake.

"No, it's okay." The reservation in her voice told me things were not okay. The uncomfortable vibe the guy gave me, mixed with her body language, had the hairs on the back of my neck prickling. Nothing felt right about the situation.

"I'd like to talk to you about the job." As I said the words, Mike seemed to perk up, and he moved closer.

She shooed him away. "Mike ... go." Without another word or look at him, she walked up the steps and into the house, put the dog down, then sat on one of the two iron chairs on the deck before staring at me.

I followed her and sat in the other chair, very aware of Mike as he wandered the yard. She'd told him to go, but he didn't listen, and everything about the situation left me uncomfortable.

"Look, I usually do the hiring for the company. Noah stepped out of line when he offered you the position." I hesitated, not sure how to tell her I wasn't on board with the hire. No matter what I said, I knew this would escalate into an all-out war with Noah, but damn it, he had no right to usurp my authority.

She blinked. "I don't understand why you'd be reticent about hiring me. I'm damned good at what I do, and I'd be a valuable asset to your team. Don't forget, I already found errors Brock missed."

She was a feisty woman, and I was stunned by her razor-sharp response. She stared back at me, unfazed and unblinking. Those big, blue-white eyes locked on me.

"Or are you looking for another reason to find fault with me?" Her chin lifted an inch, as if she was preparing to charge into battle. "I don't know what your problem is."

"Brock didn't make a mistake." False accusations hurt everyone. Brock was a good man.

She lifted her shoulders. "Numbers don't lie, Quinn." Her full lips pursed, drawing my attention to them as a sudden curiosity about what it would be like to kiss her filled me. Shoving the inappropriate thought away, I shook my head.

"Fine, the job is yours." I stood up, shaken, and finished with the conversation. "In the meantime, don't get too comfortable, Mrs. Feldspar, I'm not sure how long you'll be around."

Her cool eyes were serious as she studied me.

"Is that a threat, Mr. Lockhart?"

I snorted. "Of course not."

A smile tugged the corners of her delicious lips. "Good. I look forward to working with you. You won't be sorry you hired me."

I shook my head. "I didn't hire you. My brother did."

"I'll be the best thing that ever happened to you."

Why did her words send a tingle through my abdomen and a burn to my throat? It couldn't be attraction—it was probably indigestion. Yep, that had to be it.

CHAPTER FIVE

LAUREN

I told Mike he could stay one night. That was three nights ago.

Every morning he was up with the sun and out in his truck, pretending he just arrived. Today was Thursday, and I needed to work, but I couldn't focus while he was here.

"Hi, honey, I'm home!" He walked through the door without bothering to knock, and I glared at his hopeful expression as Fawn squealed and moved through the house like a tornado.

"Daddy!" She jumped into his arms and scrunched up her face, rubbing the tip of her nose to the end of his. Lucky raced forward, barking, ready to destroy Mike.

"Lucky, no!" I shouted at the dog as if that would stop him.

"Lauren, get that dog under control, or I swear I'll—" Mike's fury dished out a growl that challenged the dog.

"*Mike.*" My sharp tone shut him up, and he finally seemed to notice Fawn's huge eyes locked on him. Her stunned expression hurt my heart, and the sheen of tears in her eyes left no doubt she knew he'd been threatening to hurt her dog.

I scooped up Lucky, who thankfully had gone silent.

"Daddy, why are you mad at Lucky?" she asked in a pitifully thin voice.

"Don't worry, I wouldn't hurt him." He lied right to her face, but I let it go. I'd rather him lie to her about this than admit he'd punt her dog over a fence if given the opportunity. I carried Lucky to the garage and set him down. He lowered his head, and he let out a sad whimper as I whispered that we loved him and closed the door.

"Promise?" Fawn sounded skeptical, and Mike quickly reassured her.

"Pinkie promise." He offered her his little finger, and they shook on it before he lowered her to the ground. She ran off, and I scowled at him.

I needed to figure out how to get him to leave for good. My fresh start couldn't happen if he stayed. I knew better than to let him in.

I hated that he was pretending we were a couple. He lied to Quinn and said he was my husband. He tried to explain it away with a wave of his hand. Then he admitted he was jealous there were other men in my life.

He knew me well enough to know I wouldn't be comfortable kicking him out on his ear. The part that killed me was that Fawn would be hurt by all of this. She was in deep again already. Her excitement that her dad was back in her life was a complication I wasn't sure how to deal with.

Part of me wondered if staying with me was a ploy to avoid child support, which the court had ordered in the divorce.

He flashed that devilish grin. "Why are you staring at me like that?" When he took a step closer, I instinctively jumped back.

"Like what?"

"Like you want me."

Bile raced to my throat. "I'm not interested. We're divorced."

He chuckled. "We'll see."

I crossed my arms, not appreciating his words. "You need to

move on. I moved away from you for a reason. I wanted a new beginning, but I can't have one as long as you're here."

His expression tightened, and genuine hurt flashed in his brilliant eyes. "You don't pull any punches, do you?"

I leaned against the counter and stared toward Fawn's room. "We both know honesty is part of who I am. I won't pretend everything's okay, even if that's your plan. I'm genuinely sorry the water main broke outside your place, but you can't stay with me."

"I know." His quiet voice surprised me. "I guess I hoped—"

"Don't." I shook my head. "It's too late. There's no working it out. No second chances. No starting over as a couple. We're through, and that's how it has to be for my sanity and hers." I jerked my chin toward Fawn's room.

"What do you mean? I'm a good dad."

I squeezed my eyes closed. "When you're there, sure."

"Keep the gloves above the belt, please." Despite his tone, I knew better. I wasn't punching down. I was stating the truth.

"Look, I kept the real reason we divorced from her for now. But I won't lie to her if she asks when she's older. I'm going to be honest. If you're serious about being a good dad, then I suggest you prepare for that and be there for her." I didn't hate him, but I certainly didn't love him. What he'd done was unforgivable, but maybe it said more about me than him.

Still tangled up inside, I watched Fawn peek out of her room, stare at both of us, then disappear back inside, closing the door while singing a happy song. "This is too confusing for her. It's time for you to go home. For good, okay?"

He stayed quiet a moment, then moved toward the door. "Fine. I'll leave. I'm sure I can find someone willing to take me in. Some would consider me a catch."

I nodded, but inside I was thinking he was a catch alright, but I wasn't in the market for a case of typhoid.

"Good. I'm glad that's settled." I knew he was trying to manipulate me, but I needed to stay strong for our daughter's well-being and my own. Putting his wants and needs before mine wasn't part of who I was—not anymore.

"Will you tell her you put me out in the cold, too?" A hint of anger colored his deadpan voice. But I wouldn't be dragged into this game. Besides, it had been warm, not cold.

"Just go."

He stormed out, and I walked toward the garage and opened the door to a pathetic-looking Lucky, still standing where I'd left him.

"Come on," I said.

He bolted inside, staying under my feet as I walked to the front door to lock it. The partially-open door gave me a full view of Quinn on my stoop, looking after Mike.

I sighed, my heart racing as I geared up for this mess. After our last conversation, I couldn't get him out of my head. I'd spent all night thinking up clever things I should've said to him.

"I didn't take you for a stalker."

He chuckled. "It's not something I'd put on my resume."

And we were back to resumes and employment.

"Can I help you?" I stepped out as Lucky trotted forward to sniff the blond Lockhart brother.

Lucky reared up on hind legs, planting a paw on Quinn's dark jeans, and sniffed the stranger. Quinn crouched down and reached for him, and Lucky hunkered down as Quinn slowed his movement and gently petted the dog.

From his pocket, he produced a treat. "Do you mind?" he asked, glancing up at me and squeezing the treat to show it was soft.

My heart skipped a beat as Mike slammed his car door so hard, I expected the windows to shatter. Ignoring my ex-husband, I nodded at Quinn.

"Sure."

He offered the treat to Lucky, who respectfully took it and gnawed on it.

"Oh, he does have teeth. I wasn't sure."

"Yeah, like four of them, and they all point in the wrong direction." I smiled at Quinn. Internally torn, I tried to assess the situation. Lucky hated men. Or, at least that is what I had assumed based on his behavior with Mike.

Then again, the only man Lucky interacted with was Mike. I hadn't even brought my father over, opting to visit my parents instead. Was I wrong about the dog or wrong about Quinn? They say animals are an excellent judge of character, and obviously Lucky liked Quinn.

"Look, I know you don't like me." I pinched the bridge of my nose between my thumb and forefinger as a headache nagged at me. "But I meant what I said. I'm good at my job, and I'll do right by your company. You're lucky to have me. Can we drop everything else and try to work together?"

"Yes." Quinn stood up. "But I'm keeping an eye on you because I want to make sure you're exactly who you say you are." He shook his head. "Too good to be true."

He smiled as if he were joking, but I knew he wasn't. Quinn didn't trust me and was right not to. I'd been less than transparent.

My heart sank. "What you see is what you get."

He walked around me as if sizing me up. He lowered his voice. "That ex-husband of yours ... Is he going to be a problem?"

I lifted my chin and gave my head a sharp shake. "Nope. But you might be if you keep doubting me."

A grin broke across his face. It was like storm clouds parting to allow sunshine through.

"Don't let it affect your work."

An uneasy feeling filled me. What exactly did Quinn think *affected my work?* Did he have the power to fire me if he found something he felt disqualified me?

"What did I do to make you dislike me?" I turned my head to follow him as he walked around me.

"I don't dislike you." He seemed surprised by my assessment.

"Then what's your problem?" I crossed my arms, noticing how his gaze jerked to my chest for a split second.

It hit me suddenly, this weird pull ... *he felt it too.*

He lifted both shoulders. "It's a gut feeling. You're too perfect for the job, and that makes me wary. Whatever you did to draw in my brothers, it's weird. Besides, hiring and firing are my jobs. Everything about this situation is odd, and I don't like it. I worry that whatever you're dealing with will be an issue at work, and I don't do workplace drama." He glanced at Mike, still idling in the driveway, watching us.

I opened my mouth to respond as the door cracked open. "Mommy?" Fawn asked, peeking out at me. "Where's Lucky?"

The dog rushed the narrow opening, and I smiled at her. "Go back inside, honey. I'll be there in a moment."

My heart sank as I looked at Quinn, who eyed me with suspicion. "You didn't mention a kid. What other secrets do you have?"

CHAPTER SIX

QUINN

Angie set the beers on the table as I glared at my brothers. "I'm not kidding. That woman is crazy."

Noah glanced at Bayden as if asking for help, but Ethan sat up and opened his big stupid mouth first.

"You're telling me..." he started, winking at Angie, and watching her bottom as she walked away. I wondered if anyone else knew she was pregnant. They hadn't told me, but I'd caught her holding a hand to her belly and staring out the window with a tiny smile. I wasn't stupid. I was good at what I did for the company because *I read people well.*

Max's secret? I knew about his wife and that he was sick before anyone else. And my brothers worried I couldn't keep a secret? I knew more about them than I let on. I knew Angie's little game with Bayden was to dig at Ethan. I knew Kandra and Noah were going to get back together from that first moment in the bar when they looked at one another. I understood how people thought and worked. Why did everyone talk to me like I was an idiot?

Ethan peeked at me again. "You're telling me that Lauren is crazy because she has a kid and an ex-husband?"

My brothers glanced at one another. Bayden let out a snort as he picked up his beer, lifted it in a silent toast to Roy, and then took a deep drink.

Noah rubbed a hand on his forehead, his head slightly lowered with an *I-can't-believe-I'm-listening-to-this* look on his face.

Were they all that naïve? "Yes, every woman with an ex-husband and a kid is crazy. Why else would she be divorced?" I said.

Noah's head rotated in my direction. "Oh, yeah, look at her. She'd have to be crazy for someone to leave her."

Ethan shook his head. "Sounds to me like the ex is crazy. I mean, who leaves someone like her ... and the kid too?"

"Her ex is nuts for sure, which says something about her decision-making skills," I said. "And don't forget, she has a kid; a fact she didn't mention once." I picked up my beer and downed half of it in several long gulps.

My brothers seemed to silently communicate in glances, shrugs, and slight head motions as the buzz of Roy's bar grew louder. People trickled in looking for beer and an enjoyable meal, and Angie buzzed around, lit up like a Christmas tree, while talking to everyone.

"Nor should she have to mention anything about her personal life, brother. That is private information that we have no right to," Noah stated.

He gave me the side-eye, and I blinked, pulling my attention from the room to him.

"Well, you still don't find it odd that she didn't say anything? Even if it's not part of the interview process, she still could've brought it up." Clearly, he didn't understand that it wasn't just one thing. Everything she said and did felt sneaky.

Bayden shrugged at Noah, and Ethan spoke up. "I don't see a problem with her being a single mom. That tells me she's capable of working under pressure and strong as hell."

"And good with numbers and multitasking. You know Mom will

invite her to dinner forever if she finds out she's a single mom," Bayden said as he scanned the group.

My heart sank. "Don't be an asshat and tell Mom."

Noah held up his illuminated phone with Mom's name at the top of the screen, showing he'd messaged her. "Sorry, already did." Noah fixed me with a stare that had my hackles up in an instant. "You know what makes little sense to me?"

"Life? Trusting your brother? How turkeys can drown if they look up in the rain?" I rapid-fired responses, and Bayden laughed.

"Don't worry. We'll stop you from looking up in the rain." Noah patted me on the back, and both of our other brothers made audible gobbling noises out of amusement. "None of those. It's that you were always the most reckless, fly by the seat of your pants person I know, and yet now, you're refusing to even take a chance on Lauren. I think there's something else here."

"There's nothing else." I needed to shut that thought down right now.

"He likes her." Ethan's words aggravated me.

Bayden chuckled, then stared at me as if contemplating the possibility.

"I don't like her," I said through gritted teeth before finishing my beer.

"You want her to have your babies," Bayden said, his eyes sparkling with mischief. "Oh, this is fun. Usually, you're the one dunking on us. Now we get to tease you."

"Shut up. I don't want kids." Screw them. They had no idea what they were talking about. My window for having a family shut the moment Ashley left me for the guy who was now her husband.

"Is that why you were upset to find out she had a kid? Because you don't want any?" Noah didn't bother to look at me. Instead, he squared his shoulders and took another drink of his brew while Ethan held back a grin.

"No, it's not, and this isn't the time to make stupid jokes." Couldn't they see how serious I was trying to be?

"I never thought I'd hear you say that." Ethan's expression warned that he was seconds from exploding in laughter at my expense.

How could I explain to them that she got under my skin? She had an ex and a child she didn't mention. It seemed like she was running from her previous life. But why? I had that same feeling I got when something wasn't right. It was like an allergic reaction and moved through me, itching at my insides.

I glanced at the oversized chalkboard Roy had put up, trying to see the soup of the day. Clam chowder ... Roy's homemade chowder could make a vegetarian choose meat.

"You guys aren't listening." If I couldn't convince them, I'd have to show them, and I'd start with that ex of hers. He seemed like bad news times a thousand.

"We're listening all right. You're coming in loud and clear." Noah's glass thumped on the wooden table. "I think—"

Noah's phone buzzed at the same time mine did, and I jolted, a terrible feeling hardening inside as Noah glanced at his device. I pulled mine from my pocket as he read his. He turned it around so I could see my mother's angry words.

Tell Quinn he'd better stop looking for trouble and instead look for a meal to take to that woman and her girl for dinner.

I checked my screen.

Quinn, leave that nice girl alone. Take her and her daughter some dinner right now, and don't you dare let me hear you using some silly reason as to why she's a poor fit. I'll box your ears, young man.

Ethan picked up his phone, then glanced at us. "You're not too old for Ma to take over her knee."

"I can't believe you texted her." I gawked at Noah while standing up. "Hiring and firing is my job. You guys agreed to let me

38

do that." I lowered my voice to an angry hiss as Norman and Ethel walked up to me.

"Thank you for hiring our granddaughter, Lauren. You'll never regret bringing her on board." Ethel pulled me into a grandmotherly hug, and Norman clapped me on the shoulder.

"We know," Noah said, smiling at me. "No regrets, right, Quinn?"

What could I say? My mother's voice echoed through my head: *leave that nice girl alone.* Her niceness wasn't the problem.

"Nope, not one regret," I lied. I had lots of regrets, but was Lauren really one of them? Maybe that was the problem. She wasn't a regret ... yet, but she could be, and that was what I was trying to avoid.

"And one of you is still single," she said, staring at me like a dieter looking in a bakery window.

"It's wonderful to see you again." I slipped away, leaving them to talk to my brothers as I headed toward the front counter.

Roy waited patiently for me to approach from the other side of the bar. "What do you think?" he asked, showing off the chalkboard. The handwriting had to be Angie's, and the little flourishes were pretty.

"It's nice— a great idea." I loved that he'd unofficially become part of the family, thanks to Angie's confusion over who her father was. Hands down, he and Max were my favorite people in town. Losing Dad was the worst thing that ever happened to me, but I had two fine gentlemen to turn to when I needed advice.

"Thank you." Roy's happy expression had me looking over my shoulder. I spied Gypsy sitting in her favorite booth, her eyes on him.

"When are you going to pop the question?" I asked. Watching their relationship grow over the last year gave me hope that maybe I had a chance of finding someone because, as bad of a match as they looked to be on the surface, they were perfect for each another.

"Soon," Roy said quietly, bringing a finger to his lips to let me know he'd brought me in on a secret that I'd take to the grave or until he shared it with the world. "What can I get you?"

I gave him my order. Well, my mother's order—food for Lauren and her daughter.

TWENTY MINUTES LATER, I left the bar with a bag of food in hand.

Only at her door did I remember shellfish allergies are a thing, and I almost walked away.

She opened her door, and her stunned expression gave way to a tight stance with her hands on her hips. Her tight black yoga pants fit like a glove, and the blue workout tank complimented her beautiful eyes. Lauren had captured her blonde hair in a sleek ponytail, and her subtle scent of clean laundry and peaches filled my lungs.

"Quinn?" Her gaze lowered to the bag in my hand but moved back to my eyes. "You're like a sticky booger that I can't shake off."

"I brought you dinner. Do you like clam chowder?" I swung the bag, hating feeling like a teenage boy with a crush. The tension mirrored my fear the first time I'd asked a girl—Mindy Cutter—to a school dance.

"I do." She narrowed her eyes. "Why are you being nice to me? I'm getting whiplash."

"My mother texted me and said you might be hungry." I wasn't ashamed to admit the truth. I may have brought food, but this wasn't a date.

Her expression softened.

"Thank you for that. Would you like to come in?" She backed up a step, and I considered what would make my mother less angry, leaving the food and dashing or making her feel welcome.

I nodded and stepped over the threshold. Closing the door, I heard her call out to her daughter as Lucky ran up to me and rolled onto his back, his tail wagging as he begged for a good petting.

"Fawn, honey, we have a guest."

"Guest?" The little girl's sweet voice brought a smile to my lips as I hunkered down and petted the dog's belly. The thump of tiny feet on the floor told me I was no longer alone, and I stayed squatted down and offered Fawn my hand.

"Hello, Fawn, I'm Quinn. It's nice to meet you." She took my hand and smiled.

"I like the name Quinn." She pointed at the bag I'd brought in. "What's that?"

"It's dinner."

Her face lit up, and she raced into the kitchen, shouting about dinner as Lucky trailed behind. I followed and smiled at Lauren's loving expression as she got her daughter ready to eat.

I saw the plates she already had out and placed the bag filled with Styrofoam containers beside them. Pulling the containers out, I set them down, and Lauren appeared at my side. "I'm not sure, but I wanted to get your okay on these." I opened the smallest container to show her the bone-shaped cookie. "Roy makes these dog cookies for pets." I opened the next container and showed her the cookie for Fawn. "Up to you." I popped the lid off the final dessert container. "I hope you like brownies." Roy's decadent brownies were the best, and I had a feeling she'd appreciate the gesture even if she didn't want the goodies. Of course, she'd have to be crazy not to like them. Then again ... wasn't that what I'd accused her of being ... crazy?

"This is so kind. What do I owe you?"

I shook my head. "It's on me."

"Because your mom texted you?" A sly smile lifted her lips.

"Yeah, my mom isn't someone I want to upset." I opened a large container filled with clam chowder and opened a bag containing still-hot bread bowls.

41

Her eyes widened at the sight of the food.

"Then I can expect niceness from you from now on?"

I nodded and leaned in. "I'm a nice guy."

"So was Ted Bundy, and you see how that turned out for those around him."

I should've been offended, but I was entertained. Lauren was funny when she wasn't trying to be. That made her trouble for me.

CHAPTER SEVEN

LAUREN

Quinn had brought treats for Lucky, Fawn, and me last night.

I sat at the table on a relaxing Friday morning with thoughts of Quinn filling my coffee-craving mind. He'd brought us dinner and refused to let me pay for the food even though I offered. And despite his gruff attitude, I swear something had thawed behind his eyes.

My electric kettle boiled, sending steam billowing into the air. I walked over to my French press coffee maker and poured the water over the grounds. The scent of coffee filled my senses, and I breathed a sigh of satisfaction before pouring a steaming mug. One thing I never skimped on was coffee beans.

I wondered if or when Quinn would show up today. Last night when he left, he'd promised there were things we needed to talk about today regarding my position, and I told him to come by anytime—I had nothing to hide, after all. Well, not much, anyway.

Wrapping my hands around the hot mug, I inhaled the steam as my mouth watered. With a splash of cream and a hint of sugar, the cup taunted me. I held back, not wanting to burn my tongue. Nothing ruined a freshly brewed cup like dead taste buds.

Instead, I headed toward the refrigerator to get Fawn's breakfast started. Typically, I'd make her oatmeal mixed with fruity yogurt and fresh berries.

I caught sight of the Styrofoam containers holding the other half of the enormous cookie Quinn had brought Fawn and the rest of the brownie I hadn't been able to eat. For me, I considered putting it in a bowl and pouring hot coffee over it, but that wouldn't serve anyone well. I'd be high on sugar and caffeine. The jitters and shakes from too much of either weren't a pretty sight.

A knock sent Lucky running for the front door. Who needed caffeine and sugar when I had a beast of a dog who made my heart slam in my chest each time he heard something?

I didn't have the time to take a second and smooth my hair. No doubt Quinn had shown up while I was a mess. It shouldn't matter what I look like in the comfort of my home, but somehow it did. For some reason, Quinn's opinion of me mattered more than the others.

Because Lucky was barking up a storm, and I didn't want him to wake Fawn, I picked him up, silencing him as I opened the door with a bright smile on my face, expecting to see Quinn.

That faded the second I laid eyes on Mike.

"Hold on," I said, moving inside and closing the front door. I walked Lucky to the garage, hating myself with every step—he deserved better. But if he bit Mike, he would either kill Lucky or force me to put him down. "I'm sorry, love. Be a good boy, okay?"

I set him down, and he stared up at me as I slowly closed the door. Anger trickled into my bloodstream as I headed to face my ex. As soon as I opened the door, he pushed his way inside.

"Alrighty then, make yourself at home," I said under my breath with as much snark as I possessed. I wasn't okay with his behavior. He had no right to be here *again*. I'd made myself clear last time we talked, and he knew better.

I followed him into the kitchen. "Why are you here?" I asked, scowling, and leaning on the doorframe as he wandered into the room.

He sighed, then ruffled the hair at the back of his head before turning to face me. "This is embarrassing." His gaze darted away, and I mentally prepared myself for whatever might come out of his mouth.

Instead of speaking, he yanked the fridge door open and peeked in the boxes. I watched as he emerged with a hunk of brownie in his hand and a ravenous expression on his face.

"What's embarrassing?" I asked, hoping to get him back on track as my blood boiled. How dare he help himself? He didn't pay for groceries, and we weren't a damn couple anymore. Why couldn't he get that through his thick skull?

He held up one finger and walked toward the counter, spied my cup of coffee, and before I could tell him no, dunked the brownie into the hot liquid. Fury tightened my fists as my nails dug half-moons into my palms.

He shoved the dripping brownie into his mouth, making a mess of my clean counters. His eyes crossed, and he let out a groan of pleasure that sent a shudder of disgust through me. "Oh, you still buy that good coffee, huh?" he said around a mouthful before picking up my mug and washing down the bite.

I gritted my teeth. His *what's mine is mine and what's yours is mine* attitude had persevered through our marriage, and I found myself simply tired of his BS.

"You came here to tell me something." The sooner he spit out why he was here, the sooner I could send him on his way.

He nodded, holding up one finger again as he finished the treat he'd snagged and chased it with my coffee. I watched his throat move as he tilted his head back, finishing the cup I'd made for myself.

Maybe it was silly, but that coffee helped me start the day with a better outlook. The ritual of making it and sipping it as I woke started my day right. Now that my ritual had been stolen from me, I was sad and angry.

He put the cup down and dragged the back of his hand along his mouth. "I was driving yesterday, and my car broke down."

My heart sank. Where exactly had he broken down that he could walk to my house? Or had he taken an Uber all the way here? And with what money?

I wished Missy was here because she'd know what to do and say. She had always warned me that I trusted Mike too quickly and didn't ask enough questions. She said by accepting everything he told me, I allowed him to take advantage of me.

Oh, I wasn't that naïve anymore. "Why are you here?" I'd give him whatever he wanted just to get rid of him.

What Missy didn't understand was how much easier it was to give in than fight. Mike was a dirty fighter, and he'd do anything to get his way. That was why he was living in our house with all our furnishings, and I was living in this small bungalow with thrift store finds. The interesting part was that I felt richer than I ever had.

He turned to face me, flashing that grin that dropped panties and made hearts melt. Heck, that smile had won me over all those years ago, until I learned who the man behind the smile truly was. By then, we had Fawn, and she became the priority.

"I just need three hundred dollars to replace the, uh, clutch." He talked fast like the brownie and coffee gave him the jolt I'd expected and avoided. I hoped it gave him heartburn and dysentery. "I know I can count on you, just like you can count on me—"

I hugged myself tightly. A fight was brewing between us, and I hated that. The one thing I'd always silently promised Fawn was to never bad mouth her father in front of her. Oh, I had plenty of things to say about the man standing in front of me, but it was important to me to let Fawn see him through her eyes and not mine. There would come a time when he'd show her who he really was, and she'd be able to make a sound judgment from her experience. In my opinion, it was always unfortunate when parents pitted their kids against the other parent.

"There's no clutch in an automatic." My firm tone seemed to change something in him. Realization filled his gaze. He knew I was on to him.

"You're right. I'm sorry. I have no idea what's wrong with the damn thing. The mechanic I went to told me he wouldn't work on it unless I could put a deposit up front, but I'm a little thin on cash right now." He stepped toward me, arms outstretched as if he wanted to pull me into a hug.

I moved away from him.

Hesitating for a second, he glanced sideways at the coffee mug he'd emptied. "And we both know you came out of the divorce better than I did."

I was frustrated that he'd try and pull that on me, but I held my tongue. Because if we got into it now, the roof would come down from all the things I wanted to yell at him.

"I'll give it to you this time, but only because I want you out of my house." I headed into my room and grabbed three hundred dollars out of the secret stash I kept for emergencies.

"It's time for you to go," I said, holding up the folded bills and walking toward the front door. He followed like Lucky did when I had a treat to offer. At the door, he hesitated, craning his neck as if looking for something ... or someone.

"You closed your bedroom door. Company?" he asked as we stepped outside.

"None of your business." I wasn't going to answer his questions about my life; I'd moved on, and he needed to do the same.

He scanned the driveway as I held up the money for him to take. "Well, no vehicles, so I guess not." With a quick motion, he plucked the money from my hand just as Quinn's truck pulled in.

I ran my fingers through my hair, and Mike's eyes narrowed. "This is the last time, okay?"

"I want to see my daughter." He planted his feet, clearly ready to start a fight. He glared at me as Quinn stepped out of his truck and walked in our direction with a comfortable, carefree stride.

"Your visitation is next weekend. Get your car fixed and have a good day." I pulled my hair into a ponytail and wished I'd done more to myself that morning than slip out of bed and dress.

Mike's eyes narrowed, but I ignored him and glanced toward Quinn, who closed the distance between us.

"Good morning," I said, praying this wouldn't become more awkward than it currently was. I didn't have the energy to fight with Mike, and I certainly couldn't pretend things were okay with Quinn. He promised to be nice to appease his mother, but I wasn't sure he thought I was cut out for the job.

"Morning." His gaze slid to Mike before meeting mine again. "Is everything okay?"

Mike narrowed his eyes. "Why wouldn't it be? Has she said something about me?"

"She hasn't said a thing, but you seem jumpy. Are you guilty of something?"

Quinn's calm tone and words brought a smile to my lips, which I struggled to stifle. Mike was guilty of a lot of things. There was the infidelity, his lying, and his taking advantage of anyone with a dollar in their pocket. Mike was just a bad excuse for a human being, but that didn't stop him from being Fawn's father. That, in and of itself, was his crowning glory. That's why I gave him the benefit of the doubt.

"I can make coffee," I said, motioning to the door.

"Are we having company?" Quinn nodded his head toward Mike without actually looking at him.

I shook my head. "No, he was just leaving." Glancing at my ex-husband and seeing the annoyance of being dismissed in his expression made the coffee and brownie issue worth every second. "Have a good day." With that, I ushered Quinn inside, closed the door, and slid the deadbolt home.

"Mom?" Fawn walked out, rubbing her eyes, and I scooped her up. "Where's Lucky?"

"In the garage."

Fawn looked at Quinn and smiled.

"Good morning," Quinn said to her with a warm grin on his face.

"Hi," she said softly before burying her head in my shoulder but not taking her eyes off him.

I understood how she felt. Quinn was one of those beautiful men who made it hard to turn away.

He reached over and tapped her chin. "I have something for you." He glanced up at me. "Do you mind?"

I shook my head, touched that he'd thought of her.

"It's still in my truck."

Fawn wriggled in my arms, trying to get down. "Can I go, Momma?" she asked.

"I'll run and get it," Quinn said.

"She can go." I trusted him. Any man that worried what his mother might think was a man I trusted to do the right thing. "Slip on shoes," I said, pressing a kiss to her forehead and setting her down.

"I don't want to." Instead, she reached her arms up at Quinn, and I watched, holding my breath as he hesitated.

Seconds later, he picked her up and walked toward the door with her perched on his hip. He talked about how tall his truck was and how she would have to be an experienced rock climber to get in.

She laughed as they left, and I walked over to let Lucky back inside. I shook my head, thinking about Quinn. He might not like me much, but he was good with my daughter.

A few moments later, they came back inside, and he held her while she held a box. Quinn opened his palm to reveal a dog treat, and I nodded, loving that he asked my permission every time. He offered it to Lucky, who'd taken up sniffing him, and it hit me: Lucky didn't bark at him once.

Quinn set Fawn on her feet and squatted down beside her. "I used to have one of these, and it was my favorite thing. Can you guess what it is?"

"What?" she asked in her sweet little voice.

"No, you have to guess. What do you think it is?"

She stared at the box for a moment, then looked up at him. "A truck?"

He held back his laugh and urged her to open the gift. She did, and I saw it was one of those stands that held the rotating planets.

"I wanted to be an astronaut when I grew up, and I loved space," Quinn told her. "See? These are all the planets." He showed her on the box. "Do you know which one is ours?"

She pointed to Earth, and pride moved through me.

"Very good." Quinn's bright tone brought a smile to her face.

"Are you an astronaut?" she asked.

He chuckled. "No, I found out I was better at socializing than dealing with space, so now I work with people, but I still help build things."

It struck me as funny that Quinn thought he was good with people, but maybe he was and it was only me he had a problem with.

"I want to be a unicorn," Fawn said with all the seriousness her voice could muster.

Quinn smiled at her. "Smart girl. Unicorns are magical and pretty and they have those amazing, twisted horns."

I considered what being a unicorn would be like and what I'd do with that horn. A giggle escaped me as I thought about shoving it up Mike's ass.

I refocused and turned to watch Quinn with my daughter. He was definitely good with kids and dogs. Everyone always said to watch how a man treated his mother and that was how he'd treat you. Mike's mother had passed years before I met him, so I had no idea how he was with her.

While that saying might be true, in my experience, it was important to look beyond that. A man should always treat his mother with respect, but it was how he treated others when no one was looking that said something about him. Watching Quinn interact with Fawn and Lucky made me wonder what kind of man he truly was. Was he the nice guy who seemed to love children and animals or the guy who didn't like me much? As if he knew I was contemplating his character, he glanced up from the toy solar system package, and his gaze met mine and something in me heated.

CHAPTER EIGHT

QUINN

When I walked outside with Fawn in my arms, her father, who was still there, glared so hard in my direction that an unsettling sensation filled me. The man rang every alarm bell in my being, and I didn't like that I'd seen her giving him money when I pulled up.

I wanted to ask questions, but I had no right.

I sat with Fawn.

"What do you build?" she asked me.

"Buildings. Did you see the police station?" I asked, and she nodded, her wide eyes sparkling with excitement. "My company built that."

Fawn traced the planets on the box with her fingers.

"Say thank you, Fawn," Lauren said softly, and Fawn nodded.

"Thank you. I love this." She held the box in both hands, and I reached forward and opened it up.

"Whoa, there's more!"

Trust an innocent child to think that the box was the gift. I held back my laughter, not wanting to crush her self-esteem. "It's a model." I pulled it out, and it fell into place with the sun in the center and the long arms rotating the planets around. I demonstrated how she could gently spin it to watch them turn.

She stared, mouth ajar.

I tilted it and opened the bottom of the base and uncoiled the cord before hurrying to the wall and taking a plastic safety plug out of the outlet before I plugged it in. The sun lit up and filled the room with a soft orange glow.

"Wow..." she whispered, moving toward me, and spinning the arm.

"I'm going to get Quinn coffee. Will you be okay?" Lauren asked Fawn, who nodded, clearly mesmerized by her new toy.

Lauren nudged her chin toward the kitchen, and I followed. Noticing her French press had already been used, I spoke up.

"You don't have to make me coffee."

She flipped on the electric kettle and busied herself cleaning out the press. "I have to make me coffee, so I might as well make you some in the process."

I tried to decode her comment as she pulled the bag of beans out of the cabinet, and my jaw hit the floor. "You drink Midnight Magic too?" I loved the Portland-based company's coffee.

She stilled, then glanced at me.

"It's my favorite," she said.

"I order their beans by the box. My brothers think I'm nuts to spend so much on coffee, but there are things you don't skimp on." I couldn't believe how small the world was that we loved the same coffee company.

"I have a friend who sends it to me. Maybe I can get you a discount." She said the words so matter-of-factly that I found myself surprised.

"I don't mind paying full price. I'd rather support their business than save myself a few bucks." I had the offer to pay less back when they got their start, but I refused the owner's proposal, stating I'd rather be a loyal paying customer to remind them they were worth their price. Quality was worth paying for. As part-owner of a small business, having loyal customers was the key to success.

She laughed. "I feel the same way." Her soft voice sent tingles up my spine. "Thank you for getting that for her."

"You're welcome. I'm not just here for fun, however." At my words, her shoulders stiffened as she poured the beans into a grinder. I waited for the noise to be over before speaking again. "Given that every time I come by, or damn near close, your husband is here, I can't help but think he's going to be a problem."

Her hands stilled as the grounds trickled into the bottom of the French press. "Mike's *not* my husband."

"Maybe you need to tell him that." Clearly, the guy hadn't come to terms with his divorce, but that still made him a walking, talking, breathing red flag. I didn't deal with red flags. I kept them away from my work and personal life.

She sighed and turned to face me. "Look, my personal life is really none of your business."

I shook my head. "That's where you're wrong. If your personal life causes workplace drama, then it's my business." Her eyes narrowed as I lowered my voice. "Unless you can guarantee he won't be an issue."

"Momma!" Fawn rushed into the room with Lucky on her heels. "I'm hungry."

Lauren smiled. "I have water going for your breakfast now, sweetie." I watched as Fawn went into the fridge and grabbed blackberries and blueberry yogurt, putting them on the counter as her mother pulled a storage container of oatmeal from the cabinet.

"Are you hungry?" Fawn asked in a voice that dragged a smile out of me.

"No, thank you." She was impossibly cute with those wide eyes, soft curls, and chubby, round cheeks.

"I like to put yogurt in my oatmeal." Her serious tone made her more adorable.

"My grandmother used to do that. She also added honey to hers." Fond memories trickled back as I watched the pair make breakfast. I stood and took the kettle off the stand as it whistled, recognizing Lauren's hands were full making Fawn's breakfast.

I offered to pour the water into the oatmeal, and she gave me a tired smile.

"Can I watch cartoons and eat?" Fawn asked in that universal *I know you're going to say no* voice.

"Sure. I'll bring it out when it's ready. Go and get settled."

Fawn took off, giggling with excitement as I poured hot water into the bowl, then into the French press.

"Back to our conversation. I can't promise he won't be trouble." Her flat voice told me she was done talking about it. "Mike's a pain in the ass, and that's part of the reason I divorced him, but short of a restraining order, which would break Fawn's heart, there's not much I can do. What do you suggest?"

She pulled two mugs from the cabinet and put them on the counter with a *thunk* while I admired her boldness.

"Step down and let me hire someone better suited for the position." There was no way she'd let that fly, but I had to try.

She turned to face me, planting her hands on her hips as her expression took on a promise of battle. "I doubt you'd find someone with better credentials than me. Noah hired me for a reason. He has faith in me. Why can't you? You don't trust your brother?"

Damn, I didn't expect her to back down, but I also didn't expect her to take a shot, either. Her comment about not trusting Noah stung. Maybe I was wrong about her. The more time I spent with her and the more she spoke, the more I liked her. Her quick wit, her willingness to stand up for herself, even to me, and her sharp but fair responses were appealing.

If she protected the company half as much as she defended herself from my comments, we had nothing to worry about. "Why did Noah pick you?" I asked.

She lifted her shoulders. "Ask him. I assume it's because he knows how lucky your company is to have my talent. Which you'd know if you stopped coming at me and took the time to research who I am and what I have to offer."

I'd been researching her and knew she was highly qualified on paper.

"Why'd you leave your last job?" That question still bothered me.

She squared her shoulders. "I got divorced and needed a change of scenery."

"Why Cross Creek?"

"My grandparents live here, and I thought it would be good for Fawn to have them nearby. Plus, my best friend lives in Silver Springs." Her hands dropped away from her hips before coming up to grab her elbows in a protective gesture that a body language expert would say was a sign she was hiding something.

"Why our company?"

She scanned the room as if looking at the town beyond. "It's a small town, and nobody else is looking for someone with my skills. Do you think I'm some kind of spy or something?" She chuckled, then seemed to realize I wasn't laughing.

"I don't know what you are, but my gut says there's something you're not telling me." Her eyes narrowed, and I knew I'd hit the nail on the head.

"I need to take this to my daughter. There's cream in the fridge and sugar in the container." She grabbed the oatmeal and left the room.

What if I was wrong? What if my problem with her was the undeniable attraction that hit me like a sucker punch every time I came near her? I prepared my coffee with a touch of cream and a dash of sugar, still thinking about her. There was one more thing I needed to talk to her about, and she wasn't going to like it.

"Was there anything else you needed?" she asked, storming back into the room like a Category 5 hurricane. She was telling me I was no longer welcome, but there was another matter to discuss.

"My mother wants you to come to dinner Sunday evening with Fawn."

She stopped and stared at me as if dumbfounded.

"Another interrogation? Quite frankly, I've had enough. I've already been hired by your brother, but honestly, maybe I should wait tables at Roy's. It would be less stressful and probably more fun."

My heart sank. The thought of her going somewhere else wasn't an option. The truth hit me like a sledgehammer to the breastbone. She was right, she was qualified. My reticence didn't come from her resume. My family hired her behind my back, which pricked at my ego. Besides that, they knew she was my type, and it dug at me that they were better at picking someone for both me and the job than I was.

"No, not an interrogation. Noah told Mom you have a daughter, and she asked me to extend an open invitation. You're welcome every Sunday until forever and probably holidays too." I lifted both shoulders. "You're part of the Lockhart Construction family."

A gleam lit her eyes. "Oh, really?" She crossed her arms and gave me a look that said she was planning something, and I knew I wouldn't like it.

"Yes, really." There was no doubt she'd find a way to make me regret my mother's kindness and my stubbornness.

"We'll be there." The mischief shining in her eyes left me more than a little unsettled. My brothers were on her side. My mother was on her side. Who was on my side?

CHAPTER NINE

LAUREN

Lucky curled up under my bare feet as I sat at the table, shoving thoughts of Quinn out of my mind as quickly as they came.

I chewed on the back of the red pen I'd grabbed to mark numbers and sections I needed to look at again. When Noah sent me the financial reports for the last five years, stating I'd already caught an unpaid debt and he'd like me to double-check the rest of the numbers, I'd been thrilled.

He told me to track my hours and work from home, that he trusted me. That trust bolstered my sense of belonging with the company and left me raring to get started. Quinn might think he was good with people—and I wouldn't deny that he was good with Fawn—but Noah could give him a run for his money in public relations.

My gaze jumped back several lines, and I marked an X next to a set of numbers, then I moved down a few lines to the same purchase, same company, same amount. Marking the second set, I chewed on my pen again.

"Mommy?" Fawn woke from her nap and her sleepy voice had me glancing at her as Missy crept up behind her.

"I'm right here, honey."

"Can I go to Aunt Missy's house? She has a slide." Fawn's tiny face and pleading eyes had me looking at Missy, who lifted both shoulders and mouthed, *I don't mind.*

"Sure. Back for dinner?" I asked Fawn, who looked up at Missy.

"We can do that." Missy nodded, and I stood up and hugged my friend, thanking her for her help.

As the two filed out the front door, the overwhelming silence filled me. With a knot in my shoulders from hunkering down over the books for hours, I stared toward the bathroom, contemplating a nice bubble bath, but being naked and alone in my new house was the last thing I wanted given Mike's propensity to show up unannounced.

I lost myself in numbers, the patterns, flows, and ebbs of purchases and payments. I marked numbers that stood out and cross-referenced invoices. The truth revealed itself as I tugged thread after thread of information from what I'd been given.

I needed more coffee to deal with this.

Standing up, I rubbed the back of my neck, staring at the spreadsheets, invoices, and information neatly stacked on my table. I might have made a mistake, but I knew in my gut I hadn't. Lucky lifted his head to watch me pace back and forth, then relaxed and went back to sleep.

Noah told me to go over my findings with Quinn, so I picked up my phone and texted him. He didn't respond, and I headed into the bathroom to grab a quick shower. Lucky, the ever-faithful pup, was right on my heels.

With my phone in hand, I placed it on the bathroom counter to hear if he messaged me.

Ten minutes later, I'd scrubbed myself clean and felt more awake. Climbing out of the shower, I heard a knock at the door. Lucky roused but didn't bark, and I wondered if that was proof Quinn was there.

Are you here? I texted him.

I am, he responded.

I just got out of the shower. Give me three minutes to get dressed.

I put the phone down and rushed to my room to get clothes. Forgoing a bra, I pulled on a reasonably clean, button-down blouse in a shade of steel gray and a pair of black pants.

Moments later, I rushed to the door, running my fingers through my wet hair to make it look presentable. Lucky trotted alongside, looking up at me like I was the crazy one while his tongue mopped the floor.

On the other side of the door, Quinn stood still, his back to me as he studied something on the street.

"Hello, I wasn't expecting you. Sorry for making you wait."

He whipped around to face me. His eyes were so heated, I inhaled and took a step back, my heart racing to a gallop in my chest.

"Come in," I said, looking away and hoping my out-of-breath voice wouldn't give away the strange effect he had on my pulse.

"I didn't know you had access to our information already." Quinn's flat tone didn't faze me.

"Noah sent it over." If he was mad I started, I could only imagine how he'd feel when he learned what I uncovered. "We need to talk."

"Those words are like nails on a chalkboard." He let out a tense chuckle.

"About the numbers." I led him into the kitchen and pointed out the discrepancies I'd uncovered. "There's a supplier here that's been double charging you for ages. Here's the weird part." I ran my fingers down the column. "I can only find one invoice for each request." Something nagged at me, but I couldn't put my finger on what bothered me. Not while Quinn stood there, smelling like the ocean on a warm sunny day. And not when he tossed me a glance filled with appreciation and not agitation.

"Are you sure?" He stared at the numbers, then looked up at me. "I want to be very sure before I talk to the lawyer about this. People's reputations are at stake."

I wanted to pop him in the head. He was hell-bent on protecting Brock's reputation but didn't care that each time he questioned me, he undermined mine.

"Let me look everything over again and double-check to make sure Noah sent everything over. He also said you guys switched from physical copies to digital. Maybe numbers got messed up when the changeover occurred." I'd seen that happen before, so it was prudent to check. "I just needed you to know I found some things. There is one thing..." I knew he wouldn't like this part.

He studied me, his expression turning serious. "What?"

"I don't have access to accounts, so I can't verify anything other than the printed records, and I'm used to being able to check against existing accounts." I stared at the spreadsheets on the table, and my body tensed as I expected to come up against a wall.

"Accounts ... you mean bank accounts?" His tone took on a wary edge, and I knew he would make my work more difficult because he still didn't trust me.

"Yes, the bank accounts." I puffed out my chest, then remembered I wasn't wearing a bra, and pushing out the girls might not have been a good idea. In my mind's eye, I remembered when Quinn's gaze had dropped to my chest for a split second before he caught himself once before.

Dropping my hands to my sides, I met his gaze head-on.

"I don't have a problem with that," he said. "Do you want to look over the numbers together?"

An enormous weight lifted off my shoulders, and I stared at him.

He glanced around as if looking for something specific.

"Where's Fawn?"

"She's at my friend Missy's house in Silver Springs. She'll be back for dinner." I missed her terribly while she was gone, but I didn't mind the break to shower and work in peace. "Speaking of dinner, you're welcome to stay."

He straightened and studied me.

"You want me to stay for dinner?"

I shrugged, trying to look nonchalant, but in truth, I did want him to stay.

"I'm pretty sure I owe you a meal, anyway," I said.

He chuckled. "You don't owe me anything."

"I'd like to return the favor." I glanced away, my cheeks burning. "Besides, I'm used to cooking for two adults."

Those words didn't taste good, and a sour feeling rose in me. "I mean, not that I'm trying to say I want to replace my ex-husband with you, it's just—"

"Yes, thank you." His words cut off my sudden flow of explanations and justifications.

"What?"

"Yes, I'll stay for dinner, and thank you." He smiled, and I found myself mesmerized by his boyish good looks and incredible bright green eyes.

Before I could stop myself, I threw my arms around him, instantly becoming aware I was still braless and hugging *Quinn*.

I glanced up at him, stunned, as he looked down at me. His eyes slipped to my lips, and I knew he was a half-second away from kissing me.

Lucky stood and clicked out of the room at a fast trot as my heart thundered, and Quinn seemed to contemplate pressing his lips to mine over the space of a heartbeat.

A knock at the door and Lucky's brief howl jerked me out of Quinn's grasp, and the moment passed.

"I'm not sure who that is," I said, rushing to answer it as if I couldn't put enough space between us. I opened the door to Missy and Fawn, whose face was covered in tears. I scooped Fawn up, and Missy lifted her shoulders.

"I'm sorry, she just became inconsolable." Missy's anguished voice pierced my heart.

"Maybe she's just not ready to be so far away." With everything that had happened in the last few months, Fawn's whole world had fallen apart, and this new normal wasn't normal yet. I wasn't upset.

"Thank you. Are you okay?"

Missy nodded. Her gaze traveled over my shoulder, and I glanced back to see Quinn offering Fawn a tiny stuffed unicorn.

My daughter sniffed and said the tiniest thank you I'd ever heard as she took the little creature. She had told him she wanted to be a unicorn, and I realized he must have kept that in mind while getting her the little toy.

"And who's this?" Missy asked.

I turned sideways to let her inside. I knew her, and she was sizing Quinn up. I watched as Fawn babbled about how her little unicorn would keep her safe.

"I'm Quinn, and I work with Lauren." Quinn offered his hand, and Missy looked at me. I closed my eyes and shook my head, praying she wouldn't say anything I couldn't come back from.

"The one that wants her gone, you mean?" Missy didn't back down, and Quinn eyed her with appreciation.

"I was wrong and I'm glad to have her on the team." Quinn's serious tone seemed to sway my friend, who glanced at me as if looking for confirmation.

Lucky walked up and begged for a good petting from the best-looking Lockhart brother.

Quinn hunkered down and gave Lucky some love while Missy gave me a look that clearly showed her stunned surprise that the man-hating dog didn't seem to have a problem with Quinn.

He's hot, she mouthed, and I tried to hold back a smile.

If she knew we'd almost kissed, she'd be yelling at me for being an idiot. And she'd be right because I swore off men for the foreseeable future.

CHAPTER TEN

QUINN

Nearly a week had passed since I'd talked to Lauren.

She'd told Noah she couldn't make it to Sunday dinner, and as I sat with a beer in Roy's bar, I wondered if I'd screwed things up by nearly kissing her.

"Oh, I know that look." Noah came and sat beside me, beer in hand. I hadn't noticed him come in, but no doubt the rest of my brothers would be right behind. Although, a quick scan of the bar told me they weren't there yet.

I angled my body away from him, hating that he wanted to pry. Couldn't the man let me drown my sorrows in peace? *Sorrows* might be too strong of a word. I wanted to agonize over the sudden radio silence from Lauren. It reminded me of when I'd rushed over to Ashley's and got down on one knee with a ring in hand. She said yes, and we recklessly married. Three days later I found her with someone else. A month later the marriage was annulled. That experience taught me not to dive into anything with both feet. It also taught me not to trust.

"What do you want?" I asked, sullenly watching the thousands of tiny bubbles racing to the top of my glass.

"I'm your brother and I want to help you if I can because you look miserable." Noah's calm tone almost broke me, but I knew I couldn't discuss Lauren with him, or he'd know he won.

"I'm not miserable." I was, but I wouldn't give him that satisfaction. I'd been unfair to Lauren, not because she couldn't do the job, but because I knew the minute I saw her, she'd do a job on me. She made me want to be the wild kid who followed his heart and not logic.

"Do you know why I hired Lauren?" Noah shifted in his seat and focused on his beer.

"Because you want to make me miserable?" I answered.

"Because she reminded me of someone. I think she reminds you of someone too, and that's why you're so hard on her. Look—"

"Don't you dare." If he said her name, I'd kick him square in the daddy bags. "The fact that you hired someone to torture me about my ex says a lot about you, doesn't it? I know Ashley is remarried and never coming back, but you know what?" I'd never told anyone the truth. "I'm glad she and I didn't work out because she toyed with my emotions. But I am terrified that history will repeat itself." Ashley had been a kind, wonderful young woman, or so I thought, but I wasn't enough for her. Even though she was with me, she was still looking, and she found her forever while I had been dreaming about ours. "I dodged a bullet not winding up with her."

"Not everyone is an Ashley, you know." Noah took a deep drink of his beer. "Some people know what they want out of the gate. You did, and she gave you what you wanted. The problem was what you wanted wasn't necessarily what she wanted."

I took a gulp of my drink. "I wanted her, and she wanted someone else. Who does that?"

The slight smile on his face told me he was thinking about Kandra, the love of his life. He had wanted her, and she wanted something else too, but in the end, they wound up together. I knew he'd been impressed by how much she'd grown up and how she'd become a better person with time. Sure, they had their rough spots, but mostly, they'd been happy since getting back together. Kandra was the one who got away, so he knew what he was talking about.

"A lot of people. You know, sometimes we have to suffer a little before we realize what good feels like. And speaking of good ... what's up with Lauren?"

I cocked my head. "What do you mean?"

He lifted his shoulders.

"She hasn't put in many hours this week. Adding to that, you're looking miserable. Did something happen?" Noah's point-blank question left me blinking.

"No." I shook my head. "She found something wrong with the numbers, then her daughter came home from a friend's house upset. Maybe she needed family time." As the words came out of my mouth, I was ashamed for lying because I'd nearly kissed her. That was absolutely within the bounds of *something happening*.

Noah gave me a knowing glance. "You've sure been spending a lot of time with her."

"Not for the last week." I downed the rest of my beer and shook my head at Roy as he gestured, asking if I wanted another.

"Interesting. Would you kindly do a wellness check on her? If you're not comfortable, I'll ask Miranda to go, but she might appreciate a more familiar face rather than the sheriff." Noah was clearly up to something, but I wasn't sure what.

"She knows Miranda, you know." His excuse didn't hold water, and we both knew it.

"You know what I mean. Will you do it or not?" He finished his beer and stared at me. "She's new in town and could use a friend."

"Fine. I'll do it." I pulled money out of my pocket to cover my beer and tip and left it under my glass before rising to my feet. "How's Kandra?" I asked.

My brother's eyes softened like a lovesick puppy.

"She's amazing. I hope one day you can find someone to love as much as I love her." With that, he pulled cash out for his drink and stood. "I need to get home." He patted me on the back. "Have a good night, brother."

"You too." With that, we headed for the door and parted ways for our separate vehicles.

———

TEN MINUTES LATER, I pulled into Lauren's driveway. Taking another tiny unicorn plush from the dash, I hid it in my pocket and got out of my truck, heading for her front door. I was a sucker for kids and especially Fawn, perfectly named for her doe-like eyes. It seemed like lately, everywhere I went, I came across little trinkets for her and the dog. It was like the universe was dead set on keeping them in my thoughts constantly.

Knocking at her door, I scanned for the parked vehicle that seemed so out of place last time I was here but didn't see it.

The door opened. "Quinn." She sounded stunned, and I took in the delicate dark smudges under her eyes that reminded me of bruising. Either I needed to beat the hell out of that ex-husband of hers, or she wasn't sleeping.

"Are you okay?"

She nodded. "I look terrible because I haven't been sleeping well."

"You look tired, but that's fine. Noah asked me to do a wellness check on you, or he'd send Miranda. I didn't think you'd want the sheriff knocking on your door, so here I am." I smiled at her.

Her tank top stretched tightly across her chest and showed off her slightly rounded belly.

"I'm fine. Going crazy over these numbers, but I'm fine." She seemed nervous to talk to me, and I wondered what had changed.

"Level with me; what's going on? I told Noah you might have needed family time because of Fawn coming home so upset. He said you're not reporting hours, and yet you're telling me the numbers are driving you crazy." I stepped toward her, but she stood her ground, eyeing me with a serious expression.

Then her facade dropped. Her arms fell to her sides, her shoulders drooped, and her head lowered. Without thinking about it, I moved toward her, guiding her back into her home and putting my arms around her.

She hugged me for a moment and then let go and closed the door behind me.

"Sorry. Thank you for that. I needed a hug."

"What's going on?" I asked, concerned for her well-being.

She sighed and glanced toward her daughter's room. "Her scheduled visit with her father is coming up, and it always stresses her out. She's not sleeping well, so I don't sleep well."

The need to protect Fawn rose in me. "He doesn't hurt her or anything, does he?"

She shook her head. "No, she loves him, and he's a good dad when he shows up. Last time he 'forgot' to come for her and showed up two hours late. This time she's afraid he'll forget her again. No one, especially a child, wants to feel like they aren't worth your time."

My heart ached for the little girl.

"By the way," she said, staring at me. "She's been sleeping with that little unicorn, swearing it'll protect her from monsters under the bed."

I pulled the new unicorn from my pocket and showed it to her.

She chuckled. "You're trying to buy her love, aren't you?" Her gaze studied my face, and I shook my head.

"Nah, I just remembered how my father used to come home from every trip that we couldn't join him on with a little toy or something new, and those memories are my favorites. He passed away a few years ago." A sudden ache filled my gut, and I held back that pain.

"I'm so sorry for your loss. I'm close to my parents, so I can't imagine what you're going through." Her genuine kindness brought a slight smile to my face. I followed her into the kitchen and looked over the papers she'd been working on.

"Looks like you're still working." Why wasn't she charging for hours? "Why aren't you reporting your hours?" It made little sense.

"I have done nothing other than stare at the numbers, trying to figure it all out." She seemed perplexed as she filled a glass with water. "Want anything to drink?"

I shook my head. "I called our supplier. They didn't double charge us, but I can see in the bank records that something isn't right."

"I was going to ask you about that." She leaned against the counter and tilted the glass against her lips, her delicate throat flexing as she swallowed.

Lauren was right. The numbers didn't add up. Now we needed to figure out why. "You need to report your hours so we can pay you for the work you do. Don't make me fire you."

She rolled her eyes with a grin. "Fine, I'll be more careful keeping track."

"This is a serious issue," I said, struggling to keep a firm tone.

"Oh, I'm sure." She set her glass on the counter and walked toward me as Lucky bounded in and begged for attention. I loved on him, thinking how strange it was that I didn't like small dogs much, but I looked forward to seeing this one.

"Hi, Lucky," I said, as Lauren glanced toward her daughter's bedroom door.

"He was asleep in her room, so she might wake up soon. I'm just glad she got some sleep." Her lowered voice told me she wanted her daughter to sleep longer, so I kept quiet.

I pulled a treat from my pocket and showed it to her, and, as always, she nodded her permission. I fed the dog the treat, as amused as ever by his teeth pointing out at crooked angles. He was a mess of a dog with that long, dangling tongue and one eye, but there was something undeniably charming about him.

"Thank you for being so good to us. I appreciate it." Her warm words surprised me.

"It's my pleasure. Are you going to be okay with her gone?" I hated the thought that she'd be alone and missing her daughter, and by all impressions, this divorce was new enough that she hadn't come to grips with things or become used to the separation from Fawn.

She faced me with a falsely bright smile. "I don't have a choice but to be okay."

Her words left me more determined than ever to keep an eye on her.

CHAPTER ELEVEN

LAUREN

Monday morning dawned with rain, which seemed fitting for my gray mood as I packed Fawn's bags.

"I love you, Momma." Fawn leaned into me and pressed her forehead to mine as I set her clothing on the bag and wrapped my arms around her.

"I love you too, baby deer." As her chubby little arms wound around me, I breathed a sigh of relief. Everything would be okay. She was my reason for living, for fighting as hard as I have, and also for ending things with Mike. I wanted more for her and more for me. Letting her see how he treated me would never make her the strong woman I wanted her to grow up to be.

She giggled. "I'm not a deer."

I smiled at this little ritual we started back when she discovered that a fawn was a baby deer. I'd explained to her then that I loved baby deer, and I'd named the girl I loved so much after them. Plus, it made a pretty name. "A fawn is a baby deer. You're Fawn, right?"

"Yes, but I'm a person, not a deer." The laughter in her tiny voice lifted my spirits until I realized it was the last I'd hear it until she got back in a week. With that, my mood crashed, and tears stung my eyes. I squeezed her gently, trying to hide my emotions from her.

"What's wrong, Momma?"

I smiled at her as she pulled back to look me in the face. "I'm going to miss you a ton, jellybean." I bopped her nose with the tip of my finger, and she snuggled in close again.

"I'll miss you too." She squeezed my neck, and I held on to her, hating every second she'd be gone. I knew some parents looked forward to a break from their kids, but Fawn was my world, especially now that I'd split from Mike. While I saw through his story about the water main and everything else, I knew his need to drag me back into his life would lead him to say and do whatever it took. Though I didn't want him around me, I wanted her to grow up with a father, and I'd support him being in her life until she didn't want him to be.

"I'll help pack!" Fawn let me go and walked to the neatly folded outfits I'd laid out on the bed. With careful hands, she took each stack and brought them to me to load into her bag. Working together, we got things done with laughter and smiles. She took to singing a song she'd made up, and I listened, soaking in the moment, and loving my life.

All too soon, a knock at the door ended the fun. Lucky began barking, and my heart sank. I pulled her into a hug and planted a kiss on her forehead. "Stay in here with Lucky, okay? Don't let him out."

She nodded, and I slipped out of the room, stopping the little critter from bolting to the front door. I rushed, wondering what brought Mike here so early—he wasn't due to pick Fawn up until tomorrow morning.

Pulling the door open, I slipped onto the porch and closed it behind me, hoping that would be enough to keep Lucky from losing his little doggone mind.

He stood there in jeans and a gray T-shirt, with a cardboard box in his arms. "I was cleaning and came across some of your stuff." As he offered me the box, I stared, shocked by his gesture. Mike didn't make kind gestures. Hell, Mike didn't clean. He didn't do anything that wasn't self-serving, so this was another way for him to worm his way back into my good graces.

I wouldn't let that happen. When it came to grace for Mike, I was empty.

"Thank you," I said, taking the box and setting it down. "You're not going to pick her up early, are you? We're not ready."

Instead, he surprised me. "No, I'll be here at eight tomorrow morning like we agreed. I just wanted to drop these things off in case you needed them."

"Well, thank you. What's in it?" I asked, nodding at the box.

He held up his hands in an expression of *I couldn't tell you.*

I opened the four flaps of the box, folding them back before checking out the black bag within. Inside, a triple D see-through mesh bra met my gaze, and my brows shot up. I'm barely a C cup— that wasn't mine. I shoved it aside with one hand and lifted a shirt I didn't recognize, either. And then one I did—from pictures on Facebook.

I turned to Mike, staring at him. "These aren't mine." There was no way he didn't know better. Anger drowned my organs, filling up my insides like water consuming a sinking ship. As I dug through the box, placing bras, lacy sleepwear, sexy outfits, even a freaking French maid costume on the little round table between us, I stared at him, resisting the urge to throw the box at his head.

He seemed confused. "They're not yours?"

It was a good act, but I wasn't buying it. Before I could respond, Quinn walked up, a smile on his face as if he was about to tell me this was some dumb prank show from the nineties and not real life.

"How goes it?" Quinn asked, completely ignoring Mike.

Humiliation filled me. Before he could get close enough to see the embarrassing items Mike brought, I swept them into the box, closed the flaps, and shoved it at Mike.

"These belong to your mistress," I said, trying to bring out a smile for Quinn that I was certain looked more like a gas pain.

The main reason Mike and I had split surfaced in my thoughts ... his affair. I'd sworn to myself that I wouldn't let Fawn think it was okay for a man to cheat. I'd chosen to leave him without letting him try to explain himself, without giving him another chance, and with no sign that what he'd done was anything other than unforgivable.

Fawn didn't know the truth, but I had promised Mike I wouldn't lie to her. When she was old enough to ask and mature enough to handle the answer, I'd tell her.

Quinn met my gaze head-on. "Are you okay?"

I nodded. "Have a good night, Mike." I stood and opened the front door. Some part of me wanted to stir up my ex, so I stared at Quinn, smiled, and invited him inside.

Quinn hesitated, his eyes narrowing as if he knew what I was up to, but he lifted his chin and walked past Mike, who glowered. I knew Mike hated the thought of me spending time with anyone else, but he had no hold over my life anymore and no say in who I saw or why. While I might be stupidly developing feelings for Quinn, I had no plans to do anything about them, but that was none of Mike's concern.

As I closed the door behind us, I turned in time to see Fawn's door open, and Lucky came running out.

Quinn showed me a treat, and I sighed, unable to hold back a smile. "Fine. You're going to make him fat."

"That's the goal," Quinn said without missing a beat. "When I'm through, he'll look like a watermelon with toothpicks for legs."

I laughed at the image as Fawn raced out of her room, right into Quinn's arms.

"I forgot to bring you something," he said.

"I don't care." Fawn's innocent response melted my heart as I walked toward the two. "I like you."

"I like you too," Quinn said, squatting down and putting her on her feet. "I was fibbing, though." He reached into his pocket and pulled out a brightly colored tube. "This is for you."

"What is it?" Fawn stared at him while I watched their exchange.

"Hold it up to your eye," he said, showing her how to do so. "And turn this end." He guided her other hand to the end of the tube.

"Wow!" she squealed.

She raced off, and I called out after her. "What do you say?"

Without missing a beat, she peeked her head out her door and shyly said, "Thank you," before disappearing back into her room with Lucky. Her bedroom door closed, and I heard her talking to Lucky as Quinn turned to me. In a second, I found myself wrapped up in his warm embrace.

"Honestly, now, are you okay?"

Something in his husky voice shattered through my walls, and the pain Mike inflicted on me finally erupted. Two fat tears rolled down my cheeks as I stared over Quinn's shoulder at my daughter's bedroom door. I prayed no man would ever hurt her like her father so callously hurt me.

"He brought over a box of things he said were mine. They belonged to the woman he cheated on me with." Inhaling, I felt him tense up. "That's why I divorced him. He cheated on me. I never wanted Fawn to think she should stay with someone if they did that to her." Letting the words out felt freeing. "I'm sorry I didn't do more work on the numbers. I'm just in an awful place."

"I don't give a damn about the numbers right now." Quinn squeezed me tighter, making it clear what did matter to him—*me*.

CHAPTER TWELVE

QUINN

Wrapped up in her arms with her sweet scent surrounding me, I hated how upset she was. I could feel her trembling and the need to settle everything, the way I always did—with humor—rose in me.

"This clears something up for me," I said, holding back a smile as she lifted her head to look me in the eye.

"What?" Her pretty lips seemed to beg for a kiss, but no way would I kiss her while her vulnerability showed.

"Your personal life is interfering with your ability to do your job." The second the words left my lips, her eyes narrowed. Her spine stiffened, and she pulled out of my grasp.

With a glance at her daughter's closed bedroom door, she kept her voice low and poked my chest with a finger. "I don't appreciate you coming at me right now. You showed up without calling when I'm not working. You don't get to criticize my personal life when I'm not on the clock. I set my hours, remember, and this is not company time. Which means I'm okay to make it a family time or ex-husband drama time." She poked me again. "Which I didn't ask for because I hate drama."

Trying to slow her roll, I said, "I'm kidding, Lauren."

Her anger didn't seem to cool with my words. "That's not funny."

I lifted both shoulders, giving her an innocent glance. "It's kind of funny."

The corners of her lips twitched before she regained tight control over her expression. Her voice lowered more, and she stepped closer to me. Her scent was vanilla and sugar, and it filled my lungs, making my mouth water.

"I'm so stressed I can barely see straight. I was packing for my daughter to go with Mike before he showed up to give me a box of his girlfriend's clothes, pretending they were mine." Anger filled her beautiful eyes. "Now I'm trying to figure out if he didn't know I'm not a triple D cup—"

It took everything in my power to keep my gaze on hers instead of glancing at her chest to measure, but I failed—miserably. Her breasts certainly seemed perfect, not too big, not too small—

"I'm up here, Quinn." She snapped the words at me, and I couldn't hold back a devilish grin as I met her gaze. She continued without missing a beat. "Or if he's trying to hurt me or mess with me. I haven't had time to process, and jokes are not helpful." She finally took a breath, and I held back as best I could.

"If you didn't think jokes were helpful, why'd you marry that dude in the first place?" *Way to go, Quinn. She says jokes aren't helpful, so you call her ex-husband harassing her a joke. Well done.*

Her lips trembled, and her gaze softened as the anger seemed to drain out of her body. She opened her mouth to speak, but a knock at the door stopped her. Furrowing her brows, she moved to answer it.

"It's got to be him," I said, knowing full well there would only be one person knocking: the ass who'd been trying to glare me to death since I arrived.

She opened the door, and there he stood, looking like an idiot. With a glance back at me, she let herself out onto the porch and closed the door behind her as I wandered in that direction.

There was fascinating architecture near the doorway that I needed to get a second look at, or that's what I told myself. I could hear them talking on the other side, which was a bonus.

"You want to take her early anyway?" Lauren's angry voice was low as if she didn't want Fawn to hear. I didn't blame her. I followed the heavy wooden beams across the ceiling, studying the angles of the shabby woodwork. This place had been incredible once, but disrepair and lack of updating had left it looking sad and worn. The bones were still good, and that's what mattered to me.

"Yeah, I don't want her around you and your new man." His anger shone through in his voice, and I held back a chuckle. He certainly didn't like the thought of her with anyone else. Clearly, he wanted to have his cake and eat it too ... I mean, have his girlfriend and his wife at least.

"Mike, she's been around you and your girlfriend since before we split. You can't have double standards. What—it's okay for you to move on, but it's not okay for me?" The disappointment in her voice didn't surprise me, but the fact she thought he'd moved on did—because he hadn't. That was clear in every action the man took. "Besides, Quinn is a work associate, not my lover."

Heat filled my veins at the thought of being her lover, and I tried to keep that line of thinking out of my mind as I noticed a gap between the drywall and the doorframe. I doubted it was anything serious but made a note of it all the same. Maybe I could talk to her about her plans for the house. Maybe she needed someone to help her renovate. I had no doubt my brothers wouldn't pass up an opportunity to work on a gem like this place.

Mike snorted. "Right. And Kristy is just my friend."

My assumption that Kristy was the girlfriend seemed to pan out when Lauren spoke up. "Look, I don't have to have this conversation with you. You're not taking Fawn early; she's not fully packed and—"

"If she's not packed, why are you spending time with your

boyfriend instead of getting her ready?" His voice left my knuckles itching to meet his nose.

She let out a defeated sigh. "Mike, I'm under no obligation to let you take her early, and I don't want you to. She'll be ready at the time we agreed on. Please leave." Lauren's tired attitude bothered me, but I noticed Fawn's door open, and I hurried over to keep her occupied. She didn't need to hear her parents arguing.

"Why don't we go find a snack?" I asked her. "I'm hungry." I wasn't, but I thought the kitchen would be far enough from the door to keep her little ears from hearing things she shouldn't.

She smiled and led me to the refrigerator. "Is Mommy outside fighting with Daddy?" I glanced into her solemn little face and had to make a snap decision. I could lie to her and feel like a dick or be honest with her and feel like a dick or blow her off and feel like a dick.

I settled for something in between the three. "I think they're talking. What's good to snack on in here?" I looked into her trusting little face as she smiled widely.

"I know where Mom hides the good cookies." She walked to a cabinet and pointed. I followed her and opened the door. In the back, I could see the box of Thin Mints and pulled them out. Fawn put a finger over her lips and glanced toward the front door. I made a big deal out of the cookies, taking them out of the box and placing them on a small china plate I found in the cupboard.

We shared a couple, and I had a feeling Lauren wouldn't mind that we'd gotten into the good cookies to keep Fawn from hearing her and Mike talk. "Are these your favorite cookies?" I asked her.

She nodded, thought a moment, then shook her head. "My favorite is the one you brought."

I chuckled, making a mental note to ask Roy for his cookie recipe so I could give it to Lauren to make for Fawn. "Oh, really?" I asked, smiling at her. "These are pretty good too." I wiped a mint crumb off her cheek and heard the front door open.

Fawn and I hurried to put the cookie sleeve back in the box and put it in the cabinet, but Lauren walked in on us, placed a hand on her hip, and feigned upset at catching us in the act.

"It was my idea," I said, noticing how Fawn glanced up at me, giving herself away as Lauren's grin widened. "She was just showing me where the best snacks are."

"Oh, really?" Lauren glanced at Fawn, who giggled and took off toward her room with chocolate still smudged on the corners of her lips. A moment later, Lucky's nails on the floor warned he was visiting us.

"She knows you guys fight." I said the words in a low voice for Lauren's ears only. "Just so you know." I wanted to tell her how proud I was of her for standing her ground and not letting Mike take Fawn early.

Lauren's shoulders drooped, and she leaned against the counter. "I try to keep it from her. He's such a jerk making demands he has no right making. It's like he forgets he cheated on me and blames me for the split. Was I supposed to look the other way and pretend it wasn't happening?"

How come I felt more like a friend than a boss to this woman? I didn't have this kind of relationship with any female. This reminded me more of how Max and I talked or how my brothers and I used to talk before they got married or otherwise attached.

"No, stand your ground."

"I deserve better. Fawn deserves better. He takes no personal accountability, and that drives me nuts. I don't want Fawn to go over there. I mean, what if his girlfriend is a bad influence? And what if this fight makes things worse?" Her hands were shaking, and I wanted to pull her into a hug.

"Do you think she's not safe?" That thought rattled me.

"Mike wouldn't hurt her, but the only thing I know about this other woman is that she has low standards and an interesting taste in bras." Her stab at humor fell flat, and I gave a sympathetic smile, but she wasn't looking at me. She seemed to stare into space.

"What can I do about it? He's her dad, and I can't take custody from him because he has poor taste in women."

"He can't have that bad of taste; he chose you."

"Well, everyone is entitled to a happy mistake here and there." She smiled, and it warmed my heart. "Besides, he's a good dad, so I don't want to deny Fawn access to her father. If that were to happen, she wouldn't see him for who he was, but she'd see me as a mom denying her the right to her father. I want Fawn to decide for herself when she's old enough."

"For what it's worth, I think you made the right choice." I glanced at her.

She seemed surprised. "Thank you, and I'm sorry for venting. This stays with us, right? I don't want my dirty laundry tossed all over Cross Creek. It's hard enough to make a new start. I don't need to complicate things by giving everyone a bird's-eye view of my mess of a life."

I nodded. "I won't say a word." Her secrets were her own, and I had no right to share them with anyone.

Her hand came to her forehead, and she let out a groan. "You're my boss, and I shouldn't be sharing this kind of personal stuff with you. No wonder Mike had the wrong idea about us."

Did he? There was an undeniable pull between us, even if she didn't want to admit it.

CHAPTER THIRTEEN

LAUREN

The last person I should've vented to was my boss—the same guy who reminded me that my troubles might make me a poor fit for the job. The same job that was going to keep my head above water.

What was I thinking? Clearly, I wasn't.

I couldn't shut up that one part of my brain that worried. I was sure my ex was trying to sabotage me. My boss was looking for reasons to let me loose. And like an idiot, I'd let those two at-odds parts of my life merge.

"You look upset." Quinn's gaze hadn't left my face. I must have been displaying every thought openly in my expression.

"I shouldn't have told you all of that. I'm sorry. We're work acquaintances, not friends." If I needed a friend, I could call Missy.

"I can separate my personal life and my professional relationship with you," he said.

"And you think I can't?"

"That's not what I said."

I let out a growl. "That's exactly what you said. You thought my struggles would impede my work. But now you're saying we could have some kind of relationship, and it wouldn't be a problem." Why did he seem to talk out of both sides of his mouth?

"There's a difference between friendship and a stressful, difficult situation like you're going through with your ex." His kind expression caught me off guard as he stood there, leaning against the worn countertop. Lucky trotted over to him and jumped up, putting a single paw on Quinn's leg as if to remind him that the dog was there.

Quinn squatted to pet the little snaggle-toothed pooch, who looked at him like he was the only person in the world. A moment later, Fawn's door opened, and she called for Lucky. The pup trotted off without hesitation, heading for his owner's room. I knew Lucky would be upset the whole time Fawn was gone because that was typical of him. He'd sleep in her bed and whimper and whine. Though he'd perk up every time he heard a vehicle drive by, only to start the process over when he realized it wasn't her.

The coming days would be a challenge, but at least I could bury myself in work. I stared at the paperwork on my table, praying I'd be able to get things done while she was gone. Being without my daughter was like being without sun.

"Thank you for your kindness." I appreciated Quinn's consideration, and I was pretty sure he said we were friends, which was nice.

Mike made friendships difficult. The only reason Missy stuck around through it all was that she knew he wanted to drive everyone away, and she refused to let him bully her into walking out of my life.

"You keep thanking me for being a decent human being. It's not a problem." Quinn pushed away from the counter to move toward the table. He sat down, shuffling through papers as if the answer to the discrepancies would reveal itself.

How could I explain what I'd been through and how I didn't expect compassion from others? I didn't want to tell him more about my life. I'd been too personal already and shared some of the most humiliating moments. Kindness was the exception in my life, not the rule. Most of the Lockharts had been nothing but kind to me. Quinn was a step behind his family, but he was getting there.

"My mother said she missed you at dinner." His words pierced my heart. "She hopes you'll come next week."

"I didn't get you in trouble for not coming, did I?" I walked over and sat down opposite him, neatly arranging the papers as he glanced at one, then another, his brow furrowed, and his attention fixed on the pages.

He looked at me over the top of one report. "Not this time. Noah stood up for you."

"Your mom seems like a formidable woman." I loved how she ran her home and how her sons wouldn't dare do anything she didn't consider respectable. She raised them to be good men, and the world needed more of that.

"She's a sweetheart. I never want to do anything to disappoint her." He gathered up a stack of papers, thumbing through each until he found what he seemed to be looking for, and moved it to the top.

I stared at him, surprised, paperwork forgotten. "You talk about her as though you are afraid of her. I assumed she was the *paddle your backside* kind of parent."

He chuckled. "No, but she dragged my brother Noah by the ear once when he left Ethan tied to a tree for an afternoon over some silly squabble. I'm not afraid she'd whup me, but I'm afraid of letting her down."

I identified with that so much. "I'm the same way with my parents." Shifting in my chair, I thought of my mom and dad. "Mom and I talk every day." Thinking about the call my father and I had the day before, I couldn't hold back a smile. "My dad and I talk once a week. Yesterday we had the cutest conversation." My throat threatened to close. "He told me he listens to an old voicemail from me where I called to tell him I love him. He admitted he plays it several times a week. Because he got a new phone and can't find the voicemail, he asked if I could call and leave another like it." Warmth filled me. "So, I did. I called to leave a voicemail that said, *I just wanted to call and say I love you,* and he was so happy about it."

I smiled and then remembered Quinn had lost his father. "I'm sorry, I didn't mean to be inconsiderate. I know you must miss your father dearly."

"I enjoy hearing you talk about your family. Thank you for sharing that story with me." He set the papers down in a neat stack.

"Thank you for keeping Fawn away from the door." I knew he did that for me, and I was grateful. Fawn might know that her father and I fight, but we didn't need to do it in front of her.

"You're welcome. I guess I should get out of your hair so you can get things done. Don't hesitate to call if you need something. It doesn't matter if it's work-related or if you just need a friend." Quinn stood up, and I mirrored his motions.

"Likewise." He was turning into someone I'd like to call a friend. Someone I could depend on. He helped me protect Fawn and come to terms with my decisions. He reinforced that I'd made the right choices regarding Mike and our marriage. Missy was always in my corner and my parents had said the same, but I had to admit that it was nice hearing someone else outside my circle validate me.

Without thinking about it, I threw my arms around him and pulled him into a hug. A hug that lasted a moment or two longer than necessary. Wrapped up in his arms, I felt safe. Accepted. Cared for. All the things I had no place feeling when spending time with my boss.

I glanced at the papers as something nagged at the edges of my thoughts.

"Nobody deserves what he put you through today. Or what he put you through that ended your marriage. I hope you don't ever second guess your decisions." He tipped my chin up to give me a serious stare.

I smiled. "Thank you."

We awkwardly pulled apart as Fawn's bedroom door opened. She came rushing out as he rubbed a hand at the back of his neck, and I turned to face her as she and Lucky bounded into the room.

"Is Quinn staying for lunch?" Fawn's excitement dimmed as I shook my head.

"He has work to do, sweetheart, and I need to get you packed to go to your dad's." I cupped her chin in my hand, and she threw her arms around my hips.

"I already packed, Momma." Her sweet voice lifted my spirits, and I smiled down at her.

"Oh, really?"

She nodded as Quinn watched us. Fawn took my hand and led me into her room to show her packed bag, all ready to go. One of the little stuffed unicorns Quinn had brought her peeked out of the front. "You did a good job. Should we order pizza for lunch?"

Her shining bright eyes left no doubt that pizza was the only lunch option now that I'd said something.

"I can pick one up from Roy's for you and drop it off. Or ... he might do delivery," Quinn said.

"I don't want to bother you." I knew there were things he needed to do other than help us order and pick up pizza.

"It's no bother at all." He squatted to be face-to-face with Fawn. "What do you like on your pizza?"

"Cheese."

He chuckled. "Anything else?"

She scrunched up her face. "Crust."

This time, he let out a genuine laugh.

"She loves Canadian bacon and pineapple." I walked out of her room to get my wallet as she talked to Lucky about pizza for lunch. Quinn followed me while I pulled out cash for the pizza and handed it to him. "Thank you for this," I said.

"No problem. I'll be back soon." He left quickly, and I sat at the kitchen table. That nagging thought still hummed away in the back of my mind. Shifting through the papers, I thought about Quinn's die-hard love of Brock, their old accountant, and the double payments. I knew what the problem was, I just had to prove it.

When Quinn knocked at the door half an hour later, I called for him to come in. I stared up at him as he strolled into the kitchen, the smell of garlic and hot pizza reaching me before he did. My daughter and the dog were right on his heels.

"Quinn, I figured it out, but you won't like the truth." I stared at him as he slowly slid the boxes onto the counter, his gaze locking on mine. He held up one finger, asking for more time, and glanced down at Fawn.

"Pizza? Garlic knots?" He picked up a plate for her and added a slice and a round, perfectly browned roll. She nodded, her face shining as I stared at him.

My stomach tensed up because any mention of wrongdoing and Brock never went well for them.

He handed Fawn the plate, and I told her to watch a movie while she ate, and I'd be there in a second.

I stood up and walked toward him as he loaded up my plate and offered it to me. "Thank you. You might want to sit down."

He shook his head, closing the pizza box. "I'll be fine. What's going on?"

Only one explanation made sense. "I think Brock was embezzling.

CHAPTER FOURTEEN

QUINN

Three weeks ago, I left her house angry because she accused Brock of stealing. I'd even asked Noah to take over talking to her and look into the matter.

He had, and now I knew the truth.

Lauren was right— Brock had been embezzling.

I'd been a total asshole for leaving, and I thanked my lucky stars I hadn't said anything I couldn't come back from.

The scent of garlic filled my nose, and I thought about the garlic knots I'd brought Lauren and Fawn that day. Now Roy's seemed to mock me with that smell as I sat at a table.

I lowered my beer, and Noah nudged me, saying my name for what must have been the umpteenth time. So deep in my thoughts, I hadn't heard him before.

"Just go talk to her. I'm sorry Brock turned out to be a loser, but you need to go talk to Lauren." Noah's brotherly attitude helped put me at ease, though my thoughts remained in turmoil. Dad respected Brock, and the man had been ripping him off for years. Lauren pulled the records for the last decade, and it was obscene the amount of money he'd pilfered from people who considered him a friend. Of course, he'd gotten much, much worse when my brothers and I took over the company. And significantly worse in his final six months with us.

I'd trusted him. Dad trusted him. And the guy was a snake.

"I was wrong about Brock." I'd gone with my gut, and it had failed me, which made me doubt every decision I'd ever made when trusting anyone. "I thought I was an excellent judge of character." I finished the last of my beer, staring down into the few suds that remained on the bottom of my glass.

"Everybody screws up, man. He was good—so good he had Dad fooled." Noah slammed his glass a little too forcefully on the table, and people glanced our way. Let them stare because I didn't give a damn.

"I don't normally screw up. That's the point. Maybe I shouldn't be the one hiring people." Maybe Noah had been right to go behind my back and give Lauren the job instead of letting me give it to someone else.

"Bull. You're good with people, Quinn. You can't blame yourself. Cons get away with being cons by being so good at what they do, they don't get caught. They are master manipulators." Noah finished the last of his drink.

"I miss when we all came here together." I shoved my glass away, digging out my wallet because I knew the time had come for this little meeting to end.

"Well, I'm sure we could schedule something with the guys. Kandra already told me she doesn't mind." Noah clapped me on the shoulder with one hand.

"That's not what I meant." There were four of us, and not so very long ago, I could remember all of us sitting around these tables, drinking. But my brothers had gone off and gotten attached. In truth, I envied them, but I also felt a little sorry for myself, knowing this chapter of our lives had ended. Never again would my brothers come to Roy's for a beer without advance planning or permission from the wives.

"I know. Quinn, everything changes. It's not good or bad. It just is." Noah tousled my hair like he used to do when we were kids, and just like I used to do back then, I tilted my head back and shoved his arm away.

"Change sucks."

"Not always. I've got to get home, though. You should talk to Lauren. She knows she was right, but having you confirm it could go a long way."

With that, my older brother waved at Roy and Gypsy and walked out the door. He left crisp bills on the table, and memories of when there would be stacks of empty glasses filled me. Before Kandra came back into Noah's life, we'd all come here every day after work. We'd gravitate here when life didn't make sense, when we were pissed at the world, when Dad's passing became too much and we couldn't be alone. And now I sat ... alone.

"That's a long face." Gypsy plopped down next to me.

"Yeah, just thinking about time and how quickly it goes." I dug money out of my wallet and tucked it under the empty glass as she nodded at me.

Gypsy laughed. "Child, you have no idea. Wait until you're my age. The days fly by in a blink. Just enjoy them as much as you can, okay?"

"I'll do my best." I smiled at her and rose from my chair. "I've got to get going, Gypsy. Thanks for the little chat."

"Anytime." She stood and made her way back to her favorite booth as she and Roy traded loving glances.

I walked out and sat in my truck, staring at the warm, welcoming bar, considering another drink instead of heading to Lauren's house with my tail tucked between my legs. I heard my father's voice in my thoughts. *Part of being a good man is admitting when you're wrong.* I turned over the engine and headed for Lauren's.

The drive to her place was a blur of creeping darkness and streetlights. When I finally turned into her driveway, I sat in my truck for a moment, preparing myself. I hadn't been there since I left in anger. How would I be received?

With a deep breath, I got out of my truck and walked to the door. With a knock, I waited for the most agonizing five seconds or five years—some measure of time—until the wooden door cracked open.

I noticed her red puffy eyes and messy hair first. "Are you sick?"

She shook her head. "No, Fawn is with her dad this week." Her voice caught, and my heart clenched as if a giant hand had wrapped around it and squeezed. "He left a minute ago, said he was taking her to dinner before leaving town."

Though that detail struck me as strange, I pushed aside worry. Maybe he always told her about his plans.

"I know that makes you sad." I clasped my hands behind my back and settled into a tight stance. "Well, I have some good news, kind of."

"I could use some." The corners of her lips curved ever so slightly upward.

"You were right about everything, and I was wrong." The hardest three words in the English language had crossed my lips, and I found myself proud.

Lauren's expression dropped. "Was that hard for you to admit?"

"Not as hard as I imagined." I stepped forward. "Look, I shouldn't have walked out on you. I think I was so determined to protect my father's legacy that admitting Brock was a thief somehow made my father seem not as smart or something."

She shook her head. "No, that's not it. Your father was a wise man I'm sure, but thieves get good by practicing, and Brock mastered his trade. He was excellent at hiding his misdeeds. This is in no way a reflection of your father's ability to run his business."

I didn't have a backup plan for this response. I expected her to be angry and rage at me, but that wasn't Lauren. She gave everyone the benefit of the doubt. "No matter, you were right. That's the good news."

"It's not good news." She breathed in and let it out in a rush. "He stole from you."

She shifted, and the door closed a few inches, pushing me out in a way that seemed more symbolic than to get rid of me physically.

I sighed. "I'm sorry. I'm not good at admitting I'm wrong."

Her posture changed and her voice softened. "Why does it have to be about being right or wrong?"

I hesitated, not sure how to answer,because she was right again. My shoulders drooped, and I stood there, feeling stupid.

"Do you want to come in?" She swung the door open.

I nodded and moved toward her. The second the door closed behind me, she wrapped me in a warm hug that felt like coming home.

"I'm sorry," she whispered, holding me tightly.

"Me too." I was sorry for doubting her, for getting mad, and I was sad that she had to be alone, missing her daughter while her garbage ex-husband had her. I let out a harsh chuckle as I noticed Lucky staring at me from the doorway of Fawn's room. "I'm sorry, Lucky. I didn't bring you a treat this time."

"He liked you before you brought him treats." A genuine smile crossed her lips.

"You don't have to make me feel better." Though it was sweet of her to try.

"No, really," she said, her expression earnest. "He barks at everyone. Missy. The mailman. He goes nuts when Mike shows up at the door. He never barks at you. Even in the beginning, he didn't." The wonder in her voice lifted my spirits, and I stepped away from her to squat down and call the little dog over.

He trotted up to me, his eyes sparkling as his pointed ears tuned me in and his long tongue nearly dragged the ground. I offered him gentle pets, and he rolled onto his belly, his little stump of a tail wiggling like mad. "You're a good boy, Lucky."

"He also misses her a ton while she's gone." Her voice nearly broke. "I miss her so much it feels like I can't breathe. Sometimes I think you're right. I can't do this job. I'm too much of an emotional wreck while she's gone that I can hardly function."

I stood up and turned to her, opening my arms again. "No, you're an amazing addition to the team, and I have zero regrets about hiring you. We're lucky you happened into our lives."

She brushed aside my words with a roll of her eyes and a rude sound. "Anyone would have caught the embezzling."

Something in her tone told me there was more to her comment, but I wasn't about to dig. "Nobody else did, though. You did that. You put up with me storming out of here like a toddler having a tantrum."

A smile lit her eyes. "You were acting like a child."

I nodded. "I was. And you kept your cool like a good mom."

Her brows scrunched together, and I mentally backed up a step. "That made things weird. I'm sorry."

She laughed, her stuffed-up nose making it sound strange. "It's okay. I needed the laugh, thank you." As if she remembered she'd been sad, her eyes went watery again. "I just miss her so much."

I pulled her into a hug, clinging to her and rocking her back and forth. "You are a wonderful mom." As much as I wanted to tell her it was okay for her to have some alone time, I knew now was not the appropriate time for that conversation.

She tipped her head back to look at me, her nose red and her watery eyes tugging something deep within me.

"Thank you," she whispered as I tried to think about anything other than kissing her soft-looking lips.

"You're welcome. It's the truth, though." I couldn't stop myself from leaning in, one agonizing millimeter at a time, as she watched me come closer.

"Are you going to kiss me?" she whispered, her eyes looking deep into mine.

"Would you be okay with that?" I asked, wanting—no, *needing*—her okay before I dared touch my lips to hers.

"I—"

The shrill trill of her phone cut off the conversation, and we jerked apart like guilty teenagers busted by our parents.

CHAPTER FIFTEEN

LAUREN

Right after my phone started to ring, a pounding knock at the door sent my heart into overdrive, and I raced to it with a backward glance at Quinn. In an instant, he made his way to my side and opened the door for me as I froze in place with a knot forming in my belly.

I recognized Miranda the second I saw her face. It wasn't as if her full sheriff uniform didn't give her away. In her arms, Fawn's tearful face tore at me. My daughter leaned into me, and I reached for her, taking her weight from Miranda as Quinn spoke for me because the lump in my throat stopped me from saying a word.

"What happened?"

Miranda didn't so much as bat an eye at her brother-in-law being in my home. "Her ex skipped out on his bill at Roy's."

"Dined and ditched?" For some reason, Quinn didn't sound surprised.

Miranda nodded as I tried to calm Fawn down. Her quiet sobbing broke my heart, and she clung to my neck like she'd never let me go. At my feet, Lucky spun in circles, trying to get to his tiny upset human.

"She was at a bar?" I asked, my throat raw and burning like I'd swallowed a mouthful of shattered glass and chased it with hard alcohol.

Quinn quickly spoke up. "Roy's is more of a family restaurant than a bar, and Roy wouldn't let anything happen to her."

"Do you want a bubble bath?" I asked Fawn, who nodded. "Want to go run the water and put in the bubbles?" Her ritual would calm her down, and I knew she liked to run her bath because it gave her the chance to add as much bubble mixture as she wanted.

I put her on her feet. "Don't get in without me, okay?"

She nodded again and rushed off, with Lucky giving chase. I watched her go before turning to Miranda.

"Mike is in jail."

With a sigh, I mentally thought about how much money I had. I'd have to bail him out, not because I wanted to, but because if I didn't, he couldn't work, and he'd be living on my couch forever.

"Thank you," I said as she turned to leave.

"No problem." With that, she was down the steps and moving toward the Tahoe in the driveway. I looked at Quinn, then headed toward the bathroom to check on Fawn. When I peeked in on her, she was sitting on the floor reading the bottle ingredients to Lucky, though she was making up most of the words. The water filled the tub, and a massive mound of lavender-scented bubbles climbed the shower tiles.

"Are you okay in here?" I asked.

Fawn nodded, her tears gone, and a slight smile on her lips as she looked up at me.

"Are you ready to get in?"

With that, she nodded again, much more enthusiastically this time. I reached in and turned off the running water.

"I'm going to leave the door open, okay? You call out if you need me." She'd recently began the "need for privacy" phase, and I didn't mind so long as the door was open, and I could hear her at all times.

Since she loved singing to Lucky in the bath, I could constantly hear she was okay.

She undressed, talking to Lucky the whole time about her favorite bubbles, and I ducked out, heading back toward Quinn. He stood in the living room between the kitchen and the front door and watched me approach.

In the bathroom, Fawn took up singing, giving me cover to talk to Quinn. "I'm going to have to bail him out." The restlessness and nerves had me trembling, and I hated it as I paced, feeling at a loss. What was Mike thinking? Dine and dash? What was he, thirteen?

Quinn grabbed my shoulders in both hands and looked me in the eye. "Don't."

Stunned, I stared at him. "What do you mean, *don't?*"

Fawn's voice rose into a crescendo in the bathroom. I didn't know the song, but she liked to make them up. No doubt Lucky was entertained. I would be, under any other circumstances.

"I mean, don't bail him out."

I let out a deep exhale, expelling my breath in a sharp sound as I lowered my head and stared past him at the ground.

"Lauren, let him stew. If he thinks you'll come running when he needs help, he'll make this a habit."

That's where Quinn was wrong and right. Mike wouldn't make it a habit. It was more like I was conditioned to bail him out when life got tough or when he made stupid choices. What else could I do? "I can't just let him spend the night in jail. What about his job?" It wasn't an option.

"Why not? He wasn't thinking about his job when he did that. Hell, he wasn't thinking about anything."

"You're probably right, but I'd like to believe I'm better than him."

I pulled my phone out of my pocket and dialed. Quinn's hands were still on my shoulders, and my gaze locked on his as I answered.

"Hi, Mom. Can you take Fawn tonight? I know it's short notice—"

"Nonsense. We'll be there in forty-five minutes." She hung up, but not before I heard my dad in the background saying he loved me. I stared Quinn down as Fawn continued to sing to Lucky.

"I have to bail him out. I still have to live with myself."

I could tell he didn't understand, but it didn't matter, because I knew what I needed to do. I just didn't want to take Fawn to the police station because I didn't want her to see more than she already had. So, letting her stay with Mom and Dad seemed like a logical choice. They had everything she needed, so no need to pack another bag. Plus, she always had fun at their house.

"He's a grown man, and he's not your husband anymore." Quinn pulled me close. "Remember how you hissed those words at me with all the venom of a rattlesnake?" The reverence in his voice didn't make his comment sound like an insult. "Where's that girl? She's the one who has to be here tonight. That girl is kick ass."

"Was that ... a compliment?" I asked, surprised.

"I think so." He didn't seem sure either, and we laughed as we waited for my parents. I left his side to peek in on Fawn, who let her bath out and turned on the shower, still singing.

When my parents showed up less than an hour later, she was clean, dressed, and ready to go. Handing her over might have been the hardest thing I'd ever done, even for the night.

"Who's this?" Dad asked in a stage whisper, gesturing at Quinn.

"A work acquaintance." I sent them a text that I needed to bail Mike out of jail, and they'd both responded much the same way Quinn had but promised to keep the truth from Fawn.

"Right, a work acquaintance," Mom said, a sparkle in her eyes as Fawn clung to her.

I took my daughter for a moment, hugging her close and feeling her heartbeat against mine.

"I love you," I whispered.

"I love you too, Momma."

"I'm going to miss you. Be good for Grandma and Grandpa?" I planted a kiss on her soft velvet cheek, hating Mike for making me send her away. The cruelty of her being brought home by a cop, then having to send her to my parents' house so I could bail his dumb ass out in the morning bothered me.

"I will," she said in her high-pitched voice. "Is Daddy going to be okay?"

I nodded, squeezing her gently and pressing my cheek to hers. "Yeah, he'll be okay." My heart clenched as Quinn stood helplessly by, obviously wanting to comfort me but not wanting to make my parents suspicious. "I love you, little lady. I'll take good care of Lucky for you." I carried her toward the door even as my mom and dad offered to take her. Their expressions told me they wanted to talk me out of helping Mike, but how could I explain to Fawn when she was older that I let her father stay in jail rather than helping him?

As I watched my parents load up and drive off with my daughter, tears ran down my face, and Quinn turned to me.

"You know, you said you wouldn't lie to Fawn when she got older about the terrible things her father did. So why are you rushing to let him out? You're raising her to be responsible. This is a good lesson for her, too. Hold him accountable for his actions." His calm tone and thought-out words made far too much sense to my exhausted, sad mind.

"I know you're right, but..."

He stared at me. "But nothing. He made a choice. He decided to dine and dash and to teach your daughter that's okay. I don't know why you're rushing off to save him rather than being stark raving mad."

I hadn't thought about it like that.

Divorcing Mike was the only time in our entire relationship that I'd held him accountable for his misdeeds. Since our divorce, I'd made it a point to rescue him every chance I got, for Fawn's sake, but in the end, I wasn't protecting her, I was protecting him.

"I don't know the right answer," I said, wrapping my arms around myself as a chilly breeze swept over me.

Quinn ushered me inside the warm house and turned to face me. "I'm not sure there is one." He seemed as unsure as I felt. "But I imagine the right answer is what's best for Fawn, and I don't think that's rescuing her father all the time. He's a bigger child than she is."

"I've always helped him out of tough spots. Before, during, and after our marriage. It's like a bad habit that's hard to break." Mike had always been in some kind of trouble, and he always blamed everyone else. I quickly learned nothing was ever his fault—even when he cheated on me.

Taking responsibility wasn't his forte. I had to give Quinn credit. It might have taken him a few weeks, but he admitted being wrong and that went a long way with me.

"Maybe it's time to stop helping him out of tough spots and let him deal with his mess. You're free of him, so stop letting him back in." Quinn's reasonable words struck some chord deep within me, and a sudden sense of relief swept over me.

Quinn was right. I'd gotten free of Mike, and he was no longer my responsibility. I didn't have to bail him out of jail—I didn't owe him jack.

"You're right, Quinn Lockhart." I smiled at him. Though he'd been unwilling at first, Quinn had stuck by me once he'd settled into the idea that I wasn't going away. In the short time I'd known him, he'd become an irreplaceable part of my life—a friend. And with how much I wanted him to kiss me, there was the potential for more.

I smiled, lowering my head. Twice now, we'd been seconds from locking lips. Twice, we'd been denied by life. Maybe, just maybe, it was time to make this happen.

The light in his eyes told me he had the same idea. He leaned in, and my heart pounded. I closed my eyes, readying myself for the kiss.

His phone rang, and he let out a soft curse. "It's Noah. If I don't answer, he'll come over." With that, he took the call, and I held back a giggle at fate's refusal to let us kiss.

Noah's voice rang out on the other end.

"Is everything okay?"

Quinn winked at me. "Did Miranda call you?"

"Yeah." Noah sounded crushed.

"I think we have everything sorted out. Thank you, talk to you tomorrow." With that, he hung up and moved toward me with the force of a storm. The intensity in his eyes melted my insides. I held my breath as he came closer.

The unmistakable sound of Lucky gagging dragged me out of the moment, and I glanced at the bathroom. "Lucky, *no!*" I knew he liked to eat the bubbles after Fawn took a bath, but in the chaos, I'd forgotten to rinse the tub.

As I rushed toward the bathroom, Quinn's frustrated laughter brought a smile to my lips.

CHAPTER SIXTEEN

QUINN

Maybe the universe didn't want me kissing Lauren. I put little stock into cosmic intervention, but this seemed like something was trying to tell me that I needed to help her through her troubles before making a move.

I followed her into the bathroom, where she scooped Lucky out of the tub. Mounds of bubbles left the little dog looking more like a fluffy white sheep than a three-pound terrier.

"Guess you're getting a bath, huh?" She held him close and glanced at me. "Can you grab me one of the brown towels out of the closet and the dog shampoo?" She nudged her chin toward the hallway door, and I nodded, opening up the closet to find stacked, neatly folded towels. Pulling one of the brown ones and the shampoo from the shelf, I followed her into her bedroom. Inside her bathroom, the silicone cracked, separating the yellowed plastic tub basin from the wall and floor. The scuffed interior left me thinking about what we could accomplish with the space, given time and a budget.

She pulled the detachable showerhead down before stepping into the shower with the dog. She spoke to Lucky in low, calming tones as she turned on the water while cradling him to her hip with the other hand.

"How can I help?" I asked.

She glanced at me, her lips curving up at the corners. "Make sure he doesn't bolt?"

I nodded, feeling useless as she ran the water up to his hind leg and then to his back. "He has sensitive skin, so if he spends too much time in Fawn's bubbles, he chafes." With slow, effortless motions, she wet his fur, rinsing away the suds from Fawn's bath. I watched, mesmerized by her gentle handling of the feisty pup. Lucky seemed at ease, tilting his head back to let her spray his chest like he enjoyed the warm water.

"You're a good boy," she murmured, rubbing him behind the ears as she continued to wet him down.

I picked up the shampoo bottle.

She smiled and held out a hand while I squeezed a quarter-sized dollop into her palm before toeing off one shoe, then the other. She let me take the showerhead from her as I squeezed into the tub with them. There was ample room for both of us, but I didn't want to give Lucky room to get past me and run around the house sopping wet.

Or at least, that would be my excuse for being as close to Lauren as I could get. She lathered up her hands, then rubbed down the dog, who sat calmly. Her soothing voice continued to tell him he was a good boy, that he must have wanted a bath, and that he didn't have to eat bubbles to get clean.

With his wiry, scraggly fur all squeaky clean, he looked like a different dog. Almost normal if you ignored his unique face.

"Does he do this often?" I asked, inhaling her sweet scent.

"As often as I forget to rinse out the tub after her baths. That's why we have oatmeal soap, to keep his skin from getting irritated from the perfumes in the bubbles and over-bathing." She tilted the container toward me, and the bottle slipped between her sudsy hands and hit the tub with a thud that startled Lucky. "I'm sorry, little one," she said, picking him up and holding him to her chest as he trembled.

Seeing the opportunity, I turned the showerhead toward her and sprayed. She let out a sound somewhere between a gasp and a laugh before reaching out and snatching the showerhead from my grasp and turning it on me. I deflected as much of the spray as I could, angling my hands to make the water splash back at her.

Some water hit her square in the face, and she blinked. Huge droplets clung to her eyelashes as she laughed, still clutching the dog to her chest. Her clothes darkened with water, and Lucky squirmed as she angled the water down, giving me the chance to take it back and spray the top of her head. Her hair flattened, and strands escaped her ponytail as she sputtered. Her eyes closed as rivulets of water streamed down her face.

"Quinn!" She shoved my arm away blindly as Lucky let out a playful bark, his tail going a million miles a second. I was certain if she put him down, his tail would knock him clean over.

Her laughter met my ears, and suddenly I wanted to hear more of that sound. Pulling the shower curtain closed, I took Lucky from her and set him down, watching his tail take him out while Lauren tried to paw water out of her eyes so she could see.

"Whoa, don't open your eyes." I worried the soap would burn them. "You've got soap all over your face. Let me rinse it off."

"Okay." She squeezed her lips together.

I lifted the showerhead. "Hold your breath."

She did, and I made a quick pass across her face, rinsing away the bubbles. "Okay, you're fine."

She exhaled and offered me her hands. I rinsed them carefully, and she wiped the water from her eyes before opening them.

"Is it weird that this is fun?" she asked, gazing at me curiously. "I never had fun like this with..."

Her expression shifted. Her eyebrows shot up like a rocket, her lips twisted, and she gave a slight shake of her head as words tumbled from her lips. "I didn't mean to compare you to him, I was just saying—"

"No worries. He's your reference. That's not an insult." I smiled at her, not at all upset. I didn't want to be anything like her ex. It was more of a compliment. Still, the moment seemed to change as she thought about Mike. Thinking about him brought him into the front of her mind and all the joy and excitement faded from her eyes.

"I guess we should get out," she said in a regretful tone. She bent over and pushed water away from Lucky's fur and down his little legs to make sure there was no hint of bubbles. After turning the water off, she stood and picked up the dog. "I should've asked you for several towels." She stared at my water-logged clothes. "I can throw your clothing in the dryer."

Like my brothers, I kept a change of clothing in my truck, but I didn't mind letting her dry my clothes.

Together we left the shower, and she wrapped Lucky in the towel while I headed for the linen closet. As she walked up to me, I handed her a towel and took one for myself. "Where's the laundry room?" I asked, and she gestured down the hall. I followed her direction and pulled off my shirt, wringing it into the standing wash sink before tossing it into the dryer. Following suit with my pants, I watched her walk into the doorway, see me in my boxers, turn red and face away.

"Sorry," I said, hoping I hadn't offended her.

"Don't be, just surprised me, is all." She smiled as she turned to the right, allowing me to see her expression without her looking at me.

"I'll wrap the towel around my waist." I did so and slipped my boxers off, putting them into the dryer with the rest of my clothing.

"I'm going to change. Make yourself comfortable." She hurried off, and I tossed my socks in, checked the lint trap, and turned the dryer on.

Walking into the living room, I glanced at the chipping paint, the dim lighting, and wondered again what her plan for the place might be. Did she want to renovate? Or did she not care about the state of the home as long as it was safe for her daughter and dog?

"You seem deep in thought," she said.

I nodded. "Just thinking about this place. It does have good bones."

Her eyes scanned the ceiling and along the walls before coming back to me.

"Really?"

"Really." I moved toward her, very aware I had nothing more than a towel around my hips.

Despite her easy smile, I could see sadness behind her eyes as she ran a hand along the back of her neck. "I can't get her asking me if her daddy was going to be okay out of my head."

I knew she was talking about Fawn's question, and my chest ached for her.

"You can't protect her—or him—forever." The guy oozed awfulness, and I knew he held too much power over her. No doubt his dine and dash move was simply a ploy to make her rescue him in some stupid *pity me, poor me* mentality that might force her to realize he couldn't live without her.

"I know." She sighed, the gesture seeming to deflate her like a balloon. She sank to the armrest of the couch, staring at a spot on the floor.

"Is he the role model you want in her life?"

"He's a decent dad." The words came out without conviction and that left me wondering if she believed them or was trying to convince herself.

"A good dad wouldn't dine and ditch and get his ass thrown in jail while taking his child out to dinner." I braced, ready for her to lash out at me. She protected her ex like I protected Brock, and neither was worthy of the effort.

"I mean, he's good with her."

"Does that matter? Can you justify his actions? She was terrified coming home with Miranda." I made a mental note to let Miranda know she'd done a great job handling Fawn. I knew the sheriff didn't like children. She'd been improving, and it showed.

"He's going to be mad."

"Let him be mad. You deserve better."

I couldn't hold back; I leaned in and pressed my lips to hers as if I could make her believe me with a kiss.

CHAPTER SEVENTEEN

LAUREN

His lips met mine in a gentle, quick kiss, as if sealing his words.

He was making too much sense. Standing in my living room in nothing more than a towel, he exuded confidence, as he should with those toned abs and powerful muscles. He might not be a builder for the company, but he sure was built like one.

Everything he said rang true, but my head and heart were locked in a battle; I needed to do what was best for Fawn. Having her father in her life seemed like something important. After all, I had a good relationship with both of my parents. What would happen to Fawn if she didn't have that connection with one of the people in her life that was supposed to love her unconditionally?

"You're a million miles away, aren't you?" Quinn asked, his understanding tone leaving me feeling terrible.

"I'm sorry. I keep going back to the fact that he's her dad." Tears stung my eyes.

Quinn pulled me into his arms.

"It's not up to you to make him into the man he should already be."

Those words reverberated through me, and something inside me broke. I couldn't force Mike to be a good guy, and I certainly couldn't influence his decisions. Standing up for him when he screwed up would teach Fawn the wrong things. I left him because I didn't want her to see how he acted and think any of his actions were acceptable. Why was I fighting so hard for him?

"You're right." I smiled up at Quinn, who furrowed his brow at me.

"In my experience, when someone says that, they mean shut up," he said in that refreshingly honest way he had.

I shook my head, a smile on my lips. "I don't mean shut up. I mean, you're absolutely right. I lost sight of the reason I left him, and you reminded me ... again." Winding my arms around his shoulders, I let all the drama roll away and let the feeling this man inspired in me float to the top. "I don't want to think about Mike anymore."

His mouth curved at the corners. "Okay, what do you want to think about?"

I rose on tiptoes and pressed my lips to his.

While I'd sworn not to get attached or involved, the thing that had scared me away was the possibility of dating another man who was all wrong for me. Despite our rough start, Quinn had been taking care of Fawn and me since he came into our lives. The strange duality of his protectiveness of the company on the one hand and his protectiveness of us on the other left me understanding him better and liking him more. Quinn was an all-in man, and he didn't take loyalty or love lightly.

"What was that for?" he whispered as our lips parted a fraction of an inch.

I couldn't hold back a grin. There was just something about this Lockhart brother standing in my living room with nothing more than a towel slung low around his hips and an air of belonging in my space that felt right.

"Because I wanted to." I wanted to kiss him while focusing on nothing more than the man standing before me. No distractions. No thoughts of anyone else. Just Quinn.

He flashed a devilish grin that did funny things to my insides. "Well, if it matters, I want you to kiss me again."

"Oh, by all means then." I kissed him again.

"I don't want to let you go," he growled under his breath.

My heart stuttered. "I don't want you to let me go." I wanted more from him, and I could feel the warmth pooling low in my core. Something was about to happen, and excitement thundered through my veins as I realized he wasn't just talking about hugging me.

Quinn Lockhart was talking about sleeping with me, and I was all in.

What the heck was wrong with me?

Still, as his hands trailed down to grip my hips, I knew I needed him.

"Are you sure?" he asked.

I nodded, breathless and frozen with anticipation, knowing full well he was asking for permission to touch me. There was nothing I could imagine wanting more.

"I'm sure," I whispered as his hands cupped my bottom.

With a quick motion, he lifted me, and my thighs gripped on his hips as naturally as if we'd done this a thousand times.

His lips met mine as he carried me to my room and lowered us both onto my bed. The taste of him, warm and cool like winter mint and sweet summer air, seemed more intoxicating than any drink I'd tried, and I needed more. Something told me that once I had a taste of Quinn, the craving for him would never stop.

"Tell me if I do anything you don't like," he whispered, his towel falling away as he worked me out of my tank top.

As the air met my skin, I sighed, not realizing how much I'd missed the intimacy of being so close to someone.

Quinn watched me, his gaze intense as his lips touched my chin, sending a shiver down my spine. Seeing him so serious left my heart in overdrive and my body humming.

His lips touched the skin below my collarbone, and he moved down, taking my pants with him. The material slid down my thighs, tickling as the warmth of the fabric gave way to the cooler air and sending an army of goosebumps rising up and down my legs.

He kissed the space between my hips, then just above my right knee, the delicate touch almost ticklish as the waistband of my pants slid past my knees. The material fell away, and his hands slid up my calves, between my knees, up my swiftly parting thighs before skimming the outside of my hips as his face took on a reverent expression.

"You are beautiful," he whispered.

I couldn't hold back a smile as I opened my arms to him. He came to me gladly, the warmth of his length brushing the inside of my thigh and driving me mad.

"Protection?" The single word broke from my lips as my cheeks blazed at my inability to speak like a human.

"In my truck. Do you have anything?"

I shook my head. I'd gone off the pill after my marriage ended because there didn't seem to be a reason. I hadn't planned on having sex again.

He pulled away with a chuckle. "I'll be right back."

On a hunch, I sat up and opened the bedside table. A box with a sticky note met my gaze, and I smiled at Missy's handwriting. *Just in case you meet Mr. Right or Mr. Right Now. I'm not judging!*

I held up the box, with the sticky note facing me, and grinned. "I was wrong. Housewarming gift from a friend." I turned it around so he could read the note, and he laughed before fixing me with a serious stare.

"Which am I? Mr. Right or Mr. Right Now?" The humor in his voice prompted me to respond.

"Why do you men always try to ruin the moment with questions? Next, you'll be asking if I love you or if we're boyfriend and girlfriend."

He stood there in all his naked glory, clutching his chest as if I'd wounded him. "Well, now I have to know … are we?"

I sat up and pressed a finger to his lips as he moved closer to me. "Shh," I said before opening the box, taking out a foil-wrapped condom, and handing it to him. A moment later, we were back to kissing, and my heart danced as the stress, pressure, and fear of the day melted away.

His lips met mine, and I opened, allowing him deeper as he filled me with a gentle motion. Our tongues collided, and my hips rose, wanting more.

When I first met Quinn, I never imagined we'd be here now, connected in body and spirit.

Pleasure took over, and his motions grew more concentrated. Without warning, the world imploded. Ecstasy filled my core, tightening my belly and rippling outward toward my fingers and toes. As I held him tighter, his chest rumbled, and his body responded.

His mouth claimed mine, and my body relaxed, tingling all over. Safe in his embrace, my lips parted as every bit of me opened for him. I knew deep down that he was a good man—the man I'd always wanted in my life but never had been lucky enough to meet.

Could he be my fresh start? My chance at something new—something real?

He broke the kiss to press his lips to my forehead, my temple, my chin, the tip of my nose, then to my mouth once more. "You're incredible," he said.

My pulse slowed, though his still thundered against my chest.

"Not bad yourself," I whispered.

A grin lit up his features, and he let out a soft chuckle.

"I still don't want to let you go." His arms flexed as he readjusted his weight above me, but I held him tightly, refusing to let it be over.

"You're not hurting me." The moment was perfect, and I wanted to bask in it for as long as I could.

CHAPTER EIGHTEEN

QUINN

I held her tight, realizing what seemed so perfect was also complicated. My company employed Lauren, and I was her direct supervisor. Even though my brothers seemed to encourage it, this relationship was a human relations nightmare that I'd have to figure out soon.

The sound of Lucky's nails on the floor warned me he was incoming. He jumped on the bed, but I wasn't prepared for a cold nose on my hip, and I yelped and backed off Lauren, who giggled.

I rolled out of bed, moved toward the bathroom to clean up, and stepped into the shower to have a moment with my thoughts. I was certain she wouldn't mind.

What did this all mean? I'd sworn off relationships because people were broken and unpredictable. I didn't want to fall in love only to have my guts ripped out again.

I'd fallen head over heels for a woman once, only to lose her to another man.

"You okay in here?" Lauren's voice met my ears, and I turned to face her shadow on the other side of the curtain.

"Yeah, I'm good. I needed to clean up." I pulled the curtain back with one hand and smiled at her. She smiled back, looking sexy and shy all at once.

"Want company?" Her voice sounded like she thought I'd tell her no, but she hoped for a yes.

I struggled internally for what felt like a decade, but an answer popped out of my mouth in point two-three seconds. "That would be nice."

Why was I torturing myself? The responsible thing would be to shut this budding relationship down before either of us wound up hurt.

The curtain opened, and I watched Lucky plant his tail end firmly on the floor outside the shower, staring at us both with disapproval.

"You keep that cold nose to yourself, mister," I said, watching his ears perk up as Lauren let out a soft laugh.

"He took liberties with you. Does he owe you dinner?" she asked as we stood under the running water together.

"Maybe," I grumbled, mocking quiet outrage at the dog's rudeness.

Lauren's amusement left me hoping we could make things work. In the shower, she stood close to me, her arms circling my neck as she rested her forehead against my chest while water rained down on us. I placed one hand between her shoulder blades and the other low on the curve of her hip.

Somehow, the marks of bearing a baby made her more beautiful. She struck me as the mother nature figure in mythology, and something so wholesome about her filled me with longing for something more.

"You're so quiet." The concern in her voice left me scrambling. How did I diplomatically handle things moving forward? The more I thought, the more I realized I owed her honesty. If nothing else, I owed her that.

"I'm concerned—"

Before I could finish, she pulled back and placed a finger on my lips in an endearing fashion. "Before you say whatever you're thinking, can I ask a favor?" Her eyes moved between mine, and I nodded. She could ask. Whether I could help was another story.

"Can you just stay with me tonight? Without the stress of what happens next. Without the awkwardness. Just two people enjoying one another's company with no conditions or expectations?" She pointed between us. "We know what this is." Her soft voice and worried eyes told me she also knew this couldn't happen, and I respected her more.

I nodded. "It was perfect."

We spent the evening just existing with one another. When we finally went to bed, we reveled in one another again. Throughout the night, all she had to do was turn to me, and we'd share passion, sometimes lasting moments, sometimes what seemed like hours.

AT SIX A.M., my phone rang, and a text popped up on hers. She giggled as we rolled apart to check on our lives outside this moment.

I ignored my brother's call, reasoning I could call him back later. She sat, furiously swiping the screen in response to the text.

"My best friend wants to come for a visit today." She sounded unsure, and I wondered how many things we'd be uncertain about moving forward. This secret wouldn't be easy for either of us to keep.

We'd been overtaken by passion, and the smart thing for both of us would be to forget last night ever happened and never speak of our encounter again, but could we?

I opened my mouth to say as much, but she seemed to know already what I was about to say.

"Don't," she whispered, not looking at me as she set her phone down on the table next to her side of the bed. "I know what you're going to say, and you don't need to tell me."

She didn't seem to take things personally and understood the gravity of the situation. Still...

I turned to her. "Are you sure you don't want to talk?"

She nodded. "I don't want to talk. Any words we say will ruin the magic of what we felt." She shoved the blankets away and stood up, giving me a magnificent view of her rounded backside as she moved toward her dresser to pick out clothes for the day.

I stood and headed for the laundry room, where my clothes still sat in the dryer. I dressed quickly, my mind racing. I didn't want to walk away— I liked Lauren, but I didn't like how complicated things felt.

Getting involved with an employee was never a good idea. What if it didn't work out?

This felt like choosing between the devil and the deep blue sea. No, it felt more like choosing to lose an arm or a leg. Either way, I'd be limbless and forced to choose between two things I desperately wanted to keep.

With an annoyed shake of my head as if it would clear my thoughts, I left the laundry room, gathered my keys and phone, and made my way to her, looking for some way to say goodbye.

She stood before her mirror, applying a touch of lipstick in a natural shade that enhanced her beauty. Her eyes met mine in the mirror, and her lips parted. "Don't," she said with a little shake of her head. "No goodbyes. This doesn't need to be weird or awkward. Just ... go."

I gave Lucky a quick belly rub and headed out to my truck, praying none of her neighbors would notice or gossip. I might have been asking too much of a small town, but a man could dream.

In the truck on my way home, I called Noah back.

"Hey," he said, pleasantries out of the way. "We're all meeting up at Roy's for drinks."

"Occasion?" I asked in a flatter tone than intended.

He sounded surprised. "You wanted us all to sit down together more, and I made it happen."

Rather than explain, I simply said, "Thanks. Talk to you then," and got off the phone. At home, I did all the things I usually did, but everything seemed different somehow. The house seemed quieter. I felt more alone. And my thoughts seemed to never leave that blonde-haired bombshell and the way she'd looked up at me.

My phone dinged, and I checked the text. A stupid grin crossed my lips when I saw Lauren messaged me. Until I read the text. *Mike knows. His girlfriend bailed him out, and he saw you leave this morning. Please don't text or call until I can figure this out.*

Didn't she want my support? Why did that sting? Out the window, a motion caught my eye, and I saw Max headed to my box. Max would know what to do. Without thinking, I rushed to the front door and motioned the mail carrier in.

He walked up with a warm smile that faded as he studied my expression. "Rough night?" he asked, leaving no doubt in my mind he knew.

The second the door closed behind him, I spoke. "Her ex-husband found out about us and is going to make her life difficult."

Despite his serious air, I could hear the incredulous note in his voice. "The husband that cheated on her is giving her a hard time because she—a single woman—had relations with another man?"

I could hear how insane it sounded. "He has some weird power over her, like a freaking spell. She told me not to text or call until she can figure things out. Max, I care about this woman." I knew my actions were foolish. I had no right to her, no right to meddle in her life. Still, I worried about her and Fawn.

"Well, you're in a tough spot. I can't advocate going against her wishes and contacting her anyway." Max's kind smile didn't help me feel better about his words. I had no right to contact her after she told me not to.

"What do you think I should do?" I asked, hating the helpless feeling rising inside me.

Max lifted his shoulders. "I'm sorry, Quinn. I think you might need to give her time and space. She's a grown woman in a difficult situation."

Max was right, but I didn't like it.

"There's something else bothering you." He planted a hand on my shoulder. "Want to talk about it?"

I nodded. "It's sensitive, Max. You know she works for our company."

He nodded. "What you say here stays between us."

I knew I could trust him, and little by little, I opened up. Starting at the beginning, I told him everything. And I mean the beginning. Ashley, what she'd done. Lauren, and how she made me feel. My worry for her and her daughter and the stress of her working for us.

And as I spoke, the truth became glaringly obvious. I didn't like the realization, but I knew what I needed to do. Maybe I was making the wrong call, but it was the only call I could make, given the options I had.

I'd own my decision, no matter how things turned out.

CHAPTER NINETEEN

LAUREN

One week later...

I wasn't sure when Noah asked me to come to the new job site if I should go. He'd invited me, telling me it was good luck to have everyone in the company present at the groundbreaking.

He didn't know my track record with luck. I'd been doing my best to keep my work life and professional life separate because Mike seemed to have forgotten I was a grown woman in charge of my destiny.

Noah gave me a heads-up that non-labor personnel treated it as a dress-up occasion. I smiled in the mirror while trying to convince myself this whole groundbreaking situation would be fine, but something ate at my insides.

Mike was jealous, but I didn't understand why he thought he had any right to tell me what I could or couldn't do.

Asking Quinn to take a step back was more about me getting my head on straight than Mike's anger. But it was prudent to make a wise choice this go-around. I had Fawn to think about.

I liked Quinn, but what if things went south? What if Fawn got attached to him and we split up? What if he hurt me? My choices weren't always right, and since my heart wasn't the only one at risk, I had to be careful.

When I told Mike he didn't get to tell me who I could or couldn't see, his anger flared. He no longer could control me, and that put me in a position of power and him in a position he wasn't used to. A place where he didn't get to rule.

He'd been furious, and I could only hope he didn't do anything stupid. Well, anything *else* stupid.

"You look beautiful." Missy's adoring tone as she held Fawn brought a smile to my face. She'd been over nearly every night since I called her in tears, telling her what had happened.

I tried to keep the identity of my lover a secret, but Missy wasn't stupid. She knew me and saw right through my fibs. It didn't help that my parents kept asking about the good-looking Lockhart brother. I guess they'd been talking to my grandparents, who'd sung the praises of the highly-regarded Lockharts.

As hard as my parents were trying to push Quinn and me together, I had to keep deflecting them with excuses like we worked together, conflict of interest, professionalism, etc. I knew they were going to keep pushing because they wanted me to be happy. While I knew Quinn would make me happy, I also thought Mike would make me happy in the beginning, when our relationship was shiny and new. Everything was good when it was fresh ... fruit, veggies, and relationships.

"Thank you." The plum-colored dress fit my curves and hid my mommy belly perfectly while showing off what I felt were my good traits; wide hips, tucked-in waist, my slim shoulders. With ruffled off-the-shoulder sleeves and a slight flounce above my knee where the skirt fell, I looked nice and felt beautiful. After a touch of lipstick and some mascara, I smoothed my hair back, and Missy clucked her tongue at me.

"Leave it down."

I did as she said and let it fall around my shoulders.

"Thank you again for watching Fawn." I made a face at my daughter, who smiled at me.

"It's no problem. We're going to watch movies. It's her turn to pick." Missy poked Fawn in the ribs, and my daughter burst out laughing before trying to tickle Missy back.

"Nothing that will give her nightmares," I said.

"I promise no Freddy Krueger, boys, or drinking." Missy gave Fawn an exaggerated wink, and my daughter laughed.

"I want a drink. Can I have milk?"

Missy looked at me, her eyes sparkling with Fawn's innocent, adorable misunderstanding of what she had meant. "Sure!"

With that, my little one slid off my friend's lap and bolted toward the kitchen with Missy following close behind.

I spritzed on my perfume and gave myself one more look in the mirror. For the first time since the night we spent making love over and over, I'd come face-to-face with Quinn again. My hand trembled, and my heart fluttered like hummingbird wings.

"Everything will be fine," I said as if saying the words out loud might make me believe them.

Lucky lifted his head from the edge of my bed and yawned. He'd been sticking to my side more and more lately, and his need to protect me only made me smile. He wouldn't be able to do much if I ever needed real protection, but I admired his spirit.

"You're a good boy, Lucky," I said.

He perked up and cocked his head to the right.

"Yes, you. You're a good boy." I smiled at him, aware I was delaying the inevitable. I was stalling because seeing Quinn would only confirm the depth of my feelings.

I wanted to crawl back under the covers and stay there until another day arrived, but I was an employee of Lockhart Construction, and this was a work event I needed to attend.

Plus, it might look weird if I refused. I'd already refused dinner at the Lockhart house again, and I knew the family noted my absence. Sliding my shoes on, I headed for the kitchen to grab my purse. Fawn sat at the table, milk in hand and a smile on her face while Missy told a story of the time she milked a real cow.

"I have to go," I said, and both glanced at me.

Fawn rushed over and threw her arms around my legs in a hug. I bent down and picked her up, squeezing her tightly and reminding myself she was worth whatever I faced. When I finally set her down again, Missy looped an arm around my shoulders.

"It's going to be great."

"You're right. It's a big project which will provide more need for my services," I said, heading for the door. "Besides, I like the Lockharts."

Missy smiled. "You like Quinn."

"I cannot lie. He's ... well, he's special." The thought of seeing him sent my heart into a frenzy again, and I couldn't keep a smile from my face. I skipped like a little girl to my car.

Maybe he'd missed me too. A girl could dream, anyway.

As I drove, the sunshine splashed down between branches to leave puddles of light on the road. I thought about my future. I loved my job and the Lockhart family. Though I'd proven myself worthy of their trust, a small part of me knew if they found out the truth ... everything would unravel. I'd forged a document and lied about my past employer's recommendation. That wasn't who I was, but it was who Mike created when he got me fired. I'd do anything to make sure Fawn had what she needed, and anything included dishonesty.

The sunshine warmed up my car, and I opened the windows to let in the fresh, cool air. The beautiful day reminded me why I loved this area. The trees shivered in the wind, and the scent of water and sweetgrass filled every breath. That was what happiness smelled like. That and Quinn's cologne and Fawn's favorite bubbles. Life was nearly perfect.

There were one or two things I'd change. I wanted to see if the feelings between Quinn and me could go anywhere. While I appreciated that he'd done as I asked and hadn't reached out, a part of me wished he had. Only because I wanted to hear his voice. I craved his reassurance, his kindness, and his unwavering belief that everything would be okay.

I tried to get a grip on my thoughts as I pulled slowly onto the job site. The ground had been churned along the road, and fresh gravel covered the thick, rich earth. Several heavy-duty excavators, bulldozers, and backhoes lined the end of the parking area, and I stared at them in awe. Big machinery to do big projects. The Lockharts were a big deal, even if they were a small company.

The field beyond seemed peaceful and serene. Part of me wanted them not to destroy the tranquility, but I'd also seen the projects the Lockhart brothers took on. They made art from building materials, and no matter what they built, it would honor the natural beauty of the surroundings.

As I parked, I watched three of the brothers—Ethan, Noah, and Bayden—break from their larger group and head for me.

My heart sank. Did Quinn not show up? Had my presence torn the heart from the company? I knew Quinn was the beating heart of his late father's legacy.

I got out of my car and smiled at the men. "Am I late?" I asked, aware I'd shown up ten minutes early. I could see some people walking around and waved at Kandra, Roy, Max, and Angie. They waved back as I scanned other faces, most of which I didn't know. So many people had shown up.

Noah shook his head with a smile. "Early, actually. We're still waiting on a few. I trust the place wasn't hard to find?"

I shook my head. "Your directions were spot on."

The sound of a truck driving up and crunching across the gravel grabbed their attention, moving it to the newcomer. That was Quinn's truck. I'd know that sound anywhere.

As his door opened, I heard another vehicle pull up. The

brothers all stiffened as Quinn came walking around his truck, not seeming to notice the newcomer.

Quinn stood away from our group, refusing to meet my gaze as the newcomer slammed their vehicle door, the sound echoing like a rifle shot.

"Look at the toys." The slurred shout left me weak in the knees, and white dots swam before my eyes. As the past merged with the future, I struggled to breathe.

Mike walked around the front of the vehicles, right toward me. His eyes narrowed as he took in my appearance. I stared at the ground, silently begging him to go away and leave me alone. How many times would I have to go through this? How many times did he plan on hitting the reset button on my life?

"Who owns those beauts?" He gestured wildly at the heavy equipment.

"This is a private worksite." Noah stepped forward. "Please leave." He was clearly ready to do battle as Bayden held him back, while Ethan watched Quinn.

Mike held both hands up, stopping in his tracks. "Sorry, sorry, I just figured if she was invited to the party, I should be too."

"And you are?" Bayden asked, his tone as mocking as possible.

Mike let out a stunned snort. He pointed at Quinn. "He knows who I am."

Oh, no, what was Mike going to do right here in front of the rest of the Lockhart brothers? Was he going to tell everyone I'd been sleeping with Quinn? Obviously, Quinn didn't want to mix business and pleasure, and that's why we hadn't moved forward.

"This is my ex-husband, Mike," I said, moving toward him like I could usher him back to his car.

"Leave, or I'll never give you another dime or any help again." I hissed the words at him under my breath, but he flashed me a disgusted look.

"You trying to bribe me to leave? You're going to have to offer more than that if you catch my meaning." He winked at Noah, who clenched a fist and moved toward him. Quinn's jump forward earned him Ethan's hands to his chest, pushing him back and telling him it's not worth it.

"You need to go," Noah said.

Mike laughed. "If my wife is here, then I'm here."

"Ex-wife," I said, fed up with his crap.

"I'll call Miranda." Bayden pulled his phone out of his pocket while I watched Mike the same way I'd watch two trains about to collide—*helpless and in shock.*

What was he about to do?

CHAPTER TWENTY

QUINN

"Why are you doing this?" Lauren asked in a low whisper few could hear.

I wanted to jump to her side, but I knew better. She told me to stay away. It might drive me up the wall, but I'd respect her wishes.

Then I took in Lauren's beauty again. Her pretty dress, her sleek shoes, that effortless, breezy loveliness she exuded. Mike also seemed to enjoy looking at her, but his sleazy gaze made me want to deck him. He never deserved her, not because she was beautiful, but because of her heart and soul. Lauren was the kindest, most generous, and considerate person I'd met, and I wanted her in my life. Who cared about the logistical nightmare of her working for me? We'd figure that out.

"I can help you get back in your car." I glanced over at Max as he walked toward Mike with a smile and an undertone of warning. Seeing everyone I cared about stand up for Lauren as if she were family warmed my heart. She'd become part of our core team, despite her best efforts not to and my best efforts to keep her at a distance. What I'd learned over the last week was that distance didn't make the feeling go away.

"Hey, it's me," Bayden said into his phone. "We need a hand when you have a moment. Love you, bye." He hung up, his attention returning to the unfolding situation.

All I could think about was Lauren. Everything about her felt like home, and I'd finally discovered why things had been so weird when I'd gone back to my place a week ago after spending the night with her; I hadn't been ready to be alone again.

We left things unfinished, Lauren and me. There was more we needed to talk about, to think about, to discuss. I wanted to try for a relationship between us, fear and worry be damned. If we were together, I knew we could grow together.

How could I convince her of that when she had to deal with an ex like Mike? How could she ever trust anyone again after his behavior?

"She has you all duped, doesn't she?" Mike's laugh turned heads, though most people seemed to pretend not to notice the drama unfolding.

I recognized that this was precisely what I'd worried about when I exposed my reservations about hiring her. But now that I knew her, I wanted to protect her from him instead of protecting my own skin.

We'd weathered a lot, my family and company both. We could get through whatever ugly scene and drama her ex caused. Even if he called us out right now and told everyone I'd stayed at her place, what would it truly cost me? As a tight-knit family-run company, our rules weren't the same as some big corporations.

"Nobody wants to hear it." Noah's voice sounded furious, and a territorial, primal urge surfaced in me. She was *mine*. I should've protected her, not my brother, who was married with a baby and another due any day.

"Are you drunk?" Max's voice carried, and I wanted to clap at his subtle undermining of whatever came out of Mike's mouth. No matter what the man said, it wouldn't be credible because someone pointed out he was drunk—or drinking, at least. *Way to go, Max!*

"Maybe I'm interested in buying this..." He waved his hand toward the field. "Whatever it is."

"It's a multi-million-dollar city building." Ethan's dry tone sent nervous laughter through the group, and Mike's eyes narrowed. He wasn't getting the welcome he hoped for or expected. I braced myself, aware that a cornered dog always fought for its life. No doubt Mike would strike, but with what?

Was there anything the man could say to change anyone's mind about Lauren? Though I'd swear years had passed since Bayden's call, I knew it had only been mere moments. I struggled to resist the urge to walk up, grab Mike, stuff him into his car, and point him in another direction with a warning of bodily harm if he continued to meddle in Lauren's life ... or any of our lives.

He wasn't welcome.

Mike turned around as if thinking and walked back and forth repeatedly, then seemed to have an idea as he put one finger in the air like a light bulb had blinked on over his head, and he was showing everyone it had lit up.

With a goofy grin on his face and a strange light in his eyes, he walked back toward the edge, between the road and the worksite.

I glanced back, aware the guys were ready to work. Time was money when you have builders on the clock, but with this fiasco still uncontained, there wasn't much we could do. No way we'd start work with a drunk civilian wandering around the site. That's how companies got sued.

"Have you gotten to know my Lauren?"

"I'm not your Lauren," she said. "Go home, Mike."

He huffed. "That's part of the problem. One day I had a home and a wife and a kid and ... well, you know. And then I didn't. That's a problem for me."

Lauren stomped toward him. "You've got more problems than that. You're drunk and embarrassing yourself."

He laughed. "Me? I'm surprised they even hired you with your history. She's a liar you know."

He looked straight at me while I tried to process his words. What history? My inner voice began a rant of *I told you so. I warned you she was trouble*, but I shut that down. Lauren wasn't a liar.

Having noticed the shock on all our faces, Mike continued.

"Oh, is that a surprise?" Mike asked.

"We're not interested in your rumors or gossip. This isn't high school." Kandra's voice rang out to support Lauren, and I saw relief flash across Lauren's face.

Mike chuckled. "Oh, but this isn't high school-level gossip."

Lauren's shoulders stiffened, and I knew he had something on her. I couldn't take it anymore, so I walked toward Mike and spoke up. "It's time for you to go. The sheriff is on her way. If you leave now, you might not get arrested again." I couldn't resist that little jab. Everyone in town knew about Mike's arrest. He hadn't been hanging around for long, but thankfully, most people thought of him as a loser and Lauren was smart for getting him out of her life.

As I walked up to him, Mike shrank away as if he thought I was going to hit him. I watched as he stepped over the edge of the gravel and threw himself down with a loud shout of pain.

Just like that, the day was wasted. Money puffed into smoke before my very eyes because we were going to have to send everyone home. Our insurance had to be called, and knowing what I did about Mike, I knew things were going to get ugly.

Thankfully, we had dozens of witnesses and a call to the sheriff to cover our backsides. We'd asked him to leave, so we'd done our due diligence.

Mike's pained shout sounded fake, and I resisted the urge to roll my eyes. In the meantime, I caught sight of Bayden, who'd been holding up his phone as if recording everything. No doubt Miranda had told him to get it all in case something happened.

Lauren jumped to Mike's side as he laid down on his back in the gravel. "I thought he was going to jump me," he shouted as stunned onlookers talked in quiet voices. Lauren's confused glance met mine, then realization dawned.

"Mike, get up now. Nobody fell for your little show. Seriously, you need to leave." She reached out a hand to him, but he slapped it away.

"I'm injured. I can't feel my legs. I think I broke my back." Mike's pathetic bellowing had several people laughing behind their hands. Nobody thought he'd broken anything. He'd barely fallen. "I'm going to get a lawyer, and I'm going to sue every one of you for my pain and suffering!"

I held back an internal groan as Noah spoke to nine-one-one in a calm voice, giving them directions.

"This is all a conspiracy to silence me!" he shouted, pointing at Lauren, who backed up with a stunned expression on her face.

I braced again, ready for the truth of our relationship to come out of his mouth in front of everyone. No doubt he was working something in the background. It wouldn't have surprised me if he'd accused Lauren of being an unfit mother. It wasn't that Mike wanted custody of Fawn, he just wanted to punish Lauren for living. Definitely a guy who wanted to have his cake and eat it too.

Lauren glanced at me, her eyes filled with unshed tears. I lifted a shoulder, not worried about the fallout of the truth.

"Did she have a shining recommendation from her last job?"

To my surprise, Mike stared directly at me.

Confused, I nodded. "She did. So what?" Why was her recommendation being brought up now?

Mike chuckled as if he knew something I didn't, and an odd feeling swept over me as Lauren made another desperate attempt to silence him. "Mike, don't. Please don't do this. You don't have to do this."

Mike ignored her pleas, and I fought the urge to put some industrial-strength tape over his mouth to shut him up. Of course, I'd be lying if I said I wasn't wondering what exactly he was getting at, but something told me everything would change once he said whatever he said.

The group watched as Mike dug into his pocket and pulled out a pink bit of paper. My heart iced over as he let out a victorious bellow, held up the paper, then unfolded it and read, "Notice of termination of employment." He glanced at me, his eyes narrowing as he spoke up.

Lauren edged away from him with a look on her face like she wanted to throw herself off a cliff.

"Effective immediately, your employment will be terminated from the Law Offices of Harper and Hawking."

Lauren let out a sound that told me he wasn't being honest, but would she tell the truth? I thought about our relationship and watched Mike fold up the note and put it back in his pocket.

I reeled from what I'd heard. "You were fired?"

Mike laughed. "Inappropriate behavior." He made a crude facial expression. "You know what I mean." His eyes were on me. "Yes, you. You know exactly what I mean."

"That's not why, and you know it," Lauren said, stooping to Mike's level as the ambulance came wailing up the road. Noah made his way to Mike, no doubt wanting to be the one that spoke with him and the paramedics first.

I stood, stunned, as Lauren slipped away toward her car, tears running down her face. In a moment, she'd turned over the engine and pulled out of her spot, driving down the road as I stood struggling to process the accusations.

Had she faked her letter of recommendation?

Had she lied to Noah? To *me*?

Her old job fired her for inappropriate behavior? What the hell happened? That didn't make sense. I thought Mike would tell everyone Lauren and I slept together, not that I'd find out she'd been fired and lied about it. Never had my initial gut feeling felt more like a curse.

CHAPTER TWENTY-ONE

LAUREN

In the driver's seat of my car, I gripped the leather steering wheel so hard it squeaked.

Mike lied. How dare he say I lost my job for inappropriate behavior. That was bogus. Here I'd been, bending over backwards, trying to work with him and make our split amicable. Heck, I gave him money when he asked for it and as much extra time with our daughter as I could. Mike would never change; all he would give me were problems and grief.

Inappropriate behavior? He made it sound like I slept around. That was him ... not me. Somehow his problems became mine. He was the master of gaslighting and the real reason I'd been fired from my previous job. He kept showing up at my work, creating so much trouble and disruption that they ultimately fired me to get rid of him. Quinn's fear of him being an issue with my work wasn't unfounded. Mike was my personal *Groundhog Day* nightmare.

I turned down my street, anger invading every cell of my being. Why was he pretending I'd slept around?

The truth hit me like boiling water, scalding and painful. This was his way to get even with me for sleeping with Quinn. Now he'd sown seeds of doubt about my character with all the Lockhart brothers. He was leaving me no option but to get back together with him, or so he thought, but I'd rather poke my eyes out with a dull stick than ever allow Mike back into my life or my bed.

And Quinn, he would think I made a habit of sleeping with coworkers, which cheapened our intimacy and made our encounter ugly and shameful. My cheeks stung with tears of humiliation.

I pulled my car into my driveway, parked, and raced up the steps to the door, and burst in, listening to Lucky's toenails click on the floor as he trotted toward me. Pressing my back to the door, I slid down until I sat, and Lucky crawled into my lap.

Mike's next move would be to sue them for pain and suffering. His "fall" was fake, but there was no way he wouldn't get away with this. Mike got away with everything. He always managed to be the victim when he was actually the villain. Aching inside, I held the dog close as my tears rolled down my cheeks to drop on his wiry fur.

The molten heat of my fury filled me, and when it cooled, it was replaced by steel.

Never again would I allow Mike to ruin my life. I needed a plan because what we were doing wasn't working.

I couldn't believe he'd so efficiently wrecked my job and any chance I had of a relationship with Quinn. Some of the blame belonged on my shoulders for not being honest up front, but eventually, the truth about the letter would've come out because my conscience wouldn't let me perpetuate that lie. I should've been honest from the beginning.

My phone chimed, and my heart skipped as I picked it up and turned on the screen to check the message.

Are you okay?

Noah's text didn't help me feel better. I wanted Quinn to text, but he was right about me. He thought I was trouble, and that I'd bring drama to the company, and I did.

My baby daddy drama had potentially cost the business big

money, and I had no reason to believe he thought of me as anything other than someone who slept with everyone she worked with like Mike had claimed.

"What are we going to do, Lucky?" I'd spent most of my savings moving to Cross Creek, where I thought I'd be out of reach of Mike's drama. Living near my grandparents had been my chance at a fresh start until I stupidly opened the door for him and gave him every opportunity to prove, yet again, that he was toxic.

Lucky stared at me with his one brown eye, his tongue flopping on my arm as he sat in my lap. I hugged him close, seeking the comfort of his unconditional love as my cheeks burned with shame.

How could I go back to working for the Lockhart brothers now? How could I show my face around town? I didn't have the money to leave, but how could I stay?

As fresh tears warmed my cheeks, I sniffed and hugged my daughter's dog. Thinking about Fawn, I tried to figure out how to proceed, to build a better life for us both.

I'd ended the marriage to have the peace to raise Fawn, demonstrating for her that no man owned her, and she should never take crap or disrespect from anyone, much less a spouse. But that was what Mike had done all along. I'd taught her by example to be a doormat, but that would change. I was done being his bank. His fall back. His escape route.

Determined, I set Lucky down and stood up. Walking in circles, I tried to think, but Quinn kept derailing my thoughts. I liked him, but could what we shared be saved? Could I even face him and apologize after this humiliating moment?

Some part of me whispered that Quinn would understand. After all, he'd been vocal in his dislike of my ex, but what if Mike's words rang true to him?

What if I asked Mike to leave us alone?

I sighed.

I could ask, but I knew he wouldn't.

Maybe if I stood firm and told him we were over, that I wasn't interested in him anymore, and I was done with his BS, he'd get the hint. If he didn't, I could just stop letting him in. Stop going above and beyond for him in hopes he'd be a decent dad to Fawn.

I loved my daughter, but her father was lethal, and I was through.

"You home?" Missy snuck out of Fawn's room and tiptoed down the hallway. "We went to the park and OD'd on cookies and milk. She dropped like a rock."

"Thanks. I've got it from here."

My friend cocked her head to the side.

"You okay?"

I nodded. "Yes. I am." Saying the words strengthened me. "I think, for the first time in my life, I'm going to be okay."

"You want to talk about it?"

I shook my head. "Maybe tomorrow. Right now, I need to plan."

Missy grabbed her keys and gave me a hug before she left.

I formulated a plan going forward.

My parents had already offered to drop Fawn off and pick her up from Mike's house for our shared custody. If I cut contact with him and leaned on my parents for support, I could effectively sever his ties to me personally. He could still see Fawn and have his visitation, but he and I wouldn't speak again after this.

Pulling my phone from my pocket, I called my mom and dad.

They answered right away.

"Hi, honey." Mom's bright tone triggered my tears, and I knew I had to talk fast before my throat closed.

"Remember how you guys offered to be a go-between for Mike and me?" I paced the floor, sending Lucky into orbit as he ran circles at my feet.

"Certainly. Has the time come?" Dad's tight voice told me he knew I had serious reasons but wouldn't push me to share unless I wanted to. "Are you okay?" he asked instead.

The thought of Mike being out of my life seemed like a weight off my shoulders. "I'm okay, but I need to take you up on that. I'll send you the visitation schedule we have set up." Tears overflowed, and my voice choked up. "Thank you both so much. I love you."

"We love you too, honey."

I needed to take the next step, and that would be difficult. "I'll talk to you guys later, okay?"

"We'll be here."

We hung up, and I stared at the phone for a moment, willing myself the strength to call Mike.

SOMEONE KNOCKING JOLTED me out of my thoughts, and I hurried to the door, opening it to Max's kind face.

"Want to talk about it?" He handed me my mail, and I wondered how I'd just seen him at the job site, and now he was here delivering mail.

"I thought you were ... are there two of you?" I asked, mostly joking but unable to wrap my head around how he'd been there and now he was at my door.

He chuckled, his eyes crinkling at the corners. "Well, now you know my secret. Can you keep it?"

I made a cross-my-heart motion and nodded.

Max stood comfortably on my front step, ready to explain himself. "I stopped by the job site to take the mail to the Lockhart brothers and show my support. I still work today."

"You saw everything, right?" Shame choked my throat, and I blinked back tears, refusing to look directly at him as if that would hide my quivering chin and the looming need to cry. What did Max think of me now?

"I did. But I know men like Mike, and I don't trust a word he says or a thing he does." He put a comforting hand on my shoulder. "And I doubt anyone else believes him either."

Somehow, his words put me at ease, and I wrapped my arms around myself as Lucky trotted up, unsure of this new person. I stepped onto the porch and closed the door in case Lucky started yapping.

"Thank you." I didn't know what else to say, but I appreciated his sentiment. His hand fell away from my shoulder, and he smiled.

"You're welcome. Quinn is a good man. Stubborn. But he has a good heart. He'll come around." Max's optimism didn't touch the part of me that worried about mine and Quinn's quasi-relationship.

I sighed. "I don't know about that, but I hope you're right." I realized that the thought of moving forward without Quinn in my life *hurt*.

"I know I'm right. Remember, I've been there for all the Lockhart brothers while they fell in love. I know things will work out exactly how they're supposed to." Max's grin grew, and I found myself surprised. The mail carrier was certainly someone everyone trusted, and he'd been there for each of the brothers as they fell in love? What stories did he have to tell? Though I wanted to ask, I didn't want to invade anyone's privacy.

"I'm going to cut ties with Mike. My parents will be go-betweens, so I never have to talk with him again. Barring some emergency, of course." As I spoke, relief flowed through me.

Max hesitated. "How do you feel about that decision?"

I contemplated the question. "Relieved. If I don't do something, I'll never have peace. He'll keep breaking into my life, turning my world upside down, and then leaving me worse off than I was before."

I stood awkwardly for a moment, then motioned to the door. "Do you want to come in and talk? I could make you some killer coffee." As I said the words, my heart dropped, thinking about how

Quinn and I bonded over our mutual love of the same small coffee company.

"I'd be happy to come in, but no coffee, thanks." Max's warm tone and kind manner put me at ease.

"Tea? Wine?" I offered.

"Water is fine, thank you." He looked into the sunshine, and I turned to open my door.

"I'm not sure what my dog will think of you." I pushed inside, and Lucky met us in the living room. "Be a good boy, Lucky," I said, watching him walk up and cautiously sniff Max's shoes.

"Can I give him a treat?" Max asked, and I swear I heard Quinn's voice coming out of his mouth. Stunned, I merely nodded as Max kneeled and handed Lucky a treat. Lucky sniffed at the offering, then gingerly took it, his little tail wagging in tiny, fast motions.

I thought about how Quinn had given Lucky treats as Max glanced at me, his eyes sparkling. "Dog treats are a mailman's best friend."

I could imagine. Though I couldn't see anyone in Cross Creek having mean dogs that Max would be subjected to—everyone loved the mailman.

"Did you teach Quinn that move?" I meant it as a joke, but my tone sounded serious.

Max didn't seem to notice. "I didn't. Does he offer Lucky treats too?"

I nodded, miserable as I saw the ghost of Quinn standing up after offering a treat to Lucky then giving Fawn whatever small toy he'd brought over for her. "Yeah, he's good with Lucky and Fawn."

"And with you?" Max's knowing smile made the corners of my lips twitch.

"Yeah, he's a good man. Kind. Patient. It made me hope that maybe not all men were like Mike." He had given me that little sense of peace. My ex was the worst the world offered, while Quinn, though a pain in the ass, was an example of the good life.

CHAPTER TWENTY-TWO

QUINN

Lauren had left. Mike and Noah were long gone in the back of an ambulance. And now, the people who had milled about at the job site after the fiasco were gone, too. Only me and a handful of people remained. No doubt the stragglers were talking about what had happened.

I pulled my phone out of my pocket and sent a quick email to Lauren's previous employer, asking for a work reference. My mother walked toward me, her expression worried.

"Where's Lauren?" she asked, standing beside me to look over the ever-shrinking group of people.

"She left."

"And you didn't go after her?" Her surprised expression told me exactly what she thought I should've done.

I stared at the field that would soon be transformed into a beautiful new building, straight from the brilliant mind of Ethan, who was walking by with Angie beside him. They seemed to be discussing something serious and didn't notice us.

"This isn't some romantic comedy, Mom. I won't chase after her and stop her from getting on a plane." If it were a romantic comedy,

I'd find out that all of this was some misunderstanding, and we'd go on with our happy little lives.

A knot in my gut warned me this wasn't a mix-up.

If Mike wasn't lying, and that pink slip was real, then she'd been fired from her previous job instead of parting on good terms like she'd told me.

I didn't give a damn that Mike insinuated that she'd slept around because I knew she wasn't like that. And even if she was, it wouldn't have mattered because that was her life and that was before me. The part that bothered me was the lie.

"You're right. You're going to go after her and talk to her like an adult because this is how real-life relationships work, son." Her sharp tone told me she didn't appreciate my romantic comedy dig, and I wasn't surprised. Mom had always been a *find the problem and fix it* kind of woman. "And you're going to do so gently because she's been through a lot, right?"

Trust my mom to know how serious things had become. Keeping secrets from her wasn't possible. "She lied, Mom."

"Why do people lie, Quinn?"

"To deceive?" I didn't understand what she was asking.

"To protect themselves. And are you going to tell me you trust the man that pretended to fall and get hurt right in front of us over the woman who has given you no reason to distrust her?"

My mother had a point.

My phone chimed, and I glanced at it. It was an email notification from her previous employer, telling me she had been "regrettably let go" from her position. I looked up from my phone.

"That was her previous employer, confirming she'd been fired." I turned to my mother, who seemed to hesitate.

As she scanned the job site, I sensed there was much she wanted to say and a lot she was holding back.

"You've met Mike. If it was anyone else, would you criticize them for doing everything in their power to escape and start a new life with their child?" Her calm, matter-of-fact tone had me blinking.

"Of course not, but would you trust someone that started their relationship with you on a falsehood?" I could count on my mother to make me think and see things from different angles.

"Intentions matter. Was the intent to deceive you or harm us?"

My mother always cut to the heart of the matter. "Perhaps not, but I called this from the beginning, and nobody believed me."

Mom let out a soft sound, suspiciously like a snort. "Does being right make you feel better?"

I crossed my arms and readjusted my footing on the hard-packed gravel as a breeze kicked up, sliced through my sweater, chilling me to the bone. "No, it feels like shit that I was right."

The corners of her lips curved into a smile. "Were you right? Have you talked to her?" She brought a hand up to shield her eyes from the sunlight, and I lifted my chin.

"I don't know, and you know I haven't."

"Okay then. Now you're going to chase her down and profess your undying love, ask her to marry you, and make me some beautiful grandbabies, okay?" Mom's gaze met mine, and I shook my head.

"What do I look like? And what do you think Lauren is? A grandbaby machine for you?" I paused, disturbed by the visual image of those words.

Mom let out a laugh—a real laugh. "You need to go talk to her. She's not Ashley."

"I know." No, she wasn't Ashley. Up until the day I proposed, Ashley had told me I was the only one for her. She lied. What she meant was I was the only one for her in that moment. The next moment, she said yes to someone else. I wasn't a fan of betrayal, and that was what every lie felt like.

"You're going to have to make some tough choices."

I nodded, fully aware that things would not be simple. Did that make them any less worth doing? Could I forgive Lauren for not being honest? Did my mother's argument—intentions matter—make a difference?

"Your father always said that some people can't see the forest for the trees. Don't be that person." Mom's whimsical tone didn't escape me. She always sounded like that when thinking about him. I missed him terribly, and I knew she did too.

I remembered my father saying those words, and I leaned in close to my mother. "I never understood the phrase."

Mom glanced at me before gazing off into the trees surrounding the job site. "It was his way of reminding all of us to take the whole situation into account and not focus on a few details."

Understanding swept through me as she explained, and I knew exactly how it applied to my current situation.

"It's getting cold. You should head home." I slipped an arm around her shoulders and gave her a gentle squeeze as she leaned into me.

"Don't forget who I raised you to be and who your father wanted you to be." Mom's loving advice reminded me of all the lessons they'd taught me growing up.

"I won't. I promise." I walked her toward her car and waited as she got inside. When she drove away from the parking spot, calling out that she loved me and telling me to call her later, I waved and thought about my next step.

As I pulled into my driveway, I caught Max at my mailbox. He waved with his signature smile, and I waved back. Sliding out of my truck, I walked up to him to ask him how his day was going.

"Good, good. That job site is nice. I can't wait to see what you guys do with the space." His optimism brought a smile to my face, despite the heaviness in my heart.

"We'll do the town proud." While I wanted to talk about what he saw at the job site, I didn't want to come out and ask him what he thought. Knowing Max, he had a lot to say if I'd be patient enough to hear him out.

"I talked with Lauren." His amiable tone and how he studied me as if looking for my reaction left me aware he was basing what he said on my response.

"Is she okay?" I worried about how she might feel and if she was alright with all that had happened.

Max nodded. "As okay as she can be, I guess."

"How's Fawn?" I worried about that bright-eyed little girl and knew she might be upset after being away from her mother. There was no doubt Lauren was holding herself together to make Fawn feel better, but that wise little girl would know something was wrong.

"I didn't see Fawn."

I breathed a sigh of relief.

We stood by my mailbox in silence, listening to the birds' chatter and the wind rustle in the leaves. When he spoke, I focused on his words.

"You need to talk to her." Max shifted toward me and put a fatherly hand on my shoulder. "I won't give away her secrets. I am, however, going to tell you to reach out to her."

Some of the constriction in my chest eased, and I breathed a little easier, seeing that Max told me to talk to her and not run. So, whatever she told him, Max still thought we could work things out. I knew she was fired, but not the actual reason why. Although I didn't care about the cause. I cared about how and why she hid the truth.

"I guess the honeymoon phase is over, huh?" I smiled at Max as my phone notified me of a message with a ding. Pulling the device out of my pocket, I unlocked the screen and checked the message from Noah.

They can't find anything wrong. X-rays are clear, and nothing looks broken or injured. No redness or swelling. The doctors aren't sure why he's in as much pain as he claims to be, but they're treating him like they know him.

I wasn't surprised. No doubt he pulled this kind of garbage every chance he got.

"Good news or bad?" Max seemed to study my face hard.

"Just an update on Mike. He seems okay."

Max's forehead wrinkled in the center. "Can't say I'm surprised."

That made two of us. "Have a good day, Max, and thank you for the chat." I had some things to think about and consider. Like how I would handle this situation with Lauren. With dignity and respect and as much kindness as I could as my mother had demanded.

"You too, Quinn. You'll make the right call." Max gave me an around-the-shoulder hug, and I patted his back.

He headed to his mail truck to continue on his route while I walked inside, deep in thought.

The facts were simple: she lied to me and faked a letter of recommendation.

Intentions mattered, like my mother said. She lied to get a job with us. Perhaps she thought this was the best place to raise her daughter, and this would be the perfect forever home for them both.

Heck, if she hadn't lied, Noah likely would've hired her anyway. Her impressive credentials, sharp wit, and ability to see through the noise to get the facts made her a valuable asset to our team.

With that thought in mind, I made a plan. There were other obstacles that needed to be addressed. As much as I wanted to see her and make sure for myself that she was okay, there was something I had to do first.

Fawn's bright smile and trusting eyes filled my thoughts, and I couldn't hold back a smile as I glanced at the fun pile of toys I'd been stocking up for her.

Mom and Dad had always reminded me to keep sight of what was truly important, and that was Lauren and Fawn.

CHAPTER TWENTY-THREE

LAUREN

I wanted, more than anything, to start fresh with the Lockhart brothers, particularly Quinn.

After all, I was proud of the work I'd done by proving their previous guy was a thief. How could I not be proud that I'd saved them money and fixed issues that were causing them trouble?

I considered calling my parents again. After all, they were the people who'd gotten me through everything. My daily talks with Mom helped me keep my sanity. Talking with Dad every week kept me grounded.

Missy came by and picked up Fawn for a girls' day out. She knew I needed time to think—time to plan what my life would look like from this point forward—but my time was up. They'd be home any second.

The door opened, and my heart danced with glee. Fawn raced for me, and I met her between the kitchen and living room. She leaped into my arms, and I caught her easily, loving how she wound her arms and legs around me as if she'd never let go.

"I missed you," I whispered into her ear before planting a kiss on her cheek.

"I missed you too." She kissed me back, her warm face and sweet smell lifting my spirits. Together, she and I could get through anything. She held out her hand. "I got pink."

"Manicures ... how fancy."

Missy stuck out her foot. "Pedicures too." She looked around the room. "Do you want me to go, stay, find your wine and drink it all?" Missy's words brought a smile to my face.

"There's a sweet blush in there. Go give it a taste." I jerked my head toward the kitchen. "You're welcome to stay the night. I might need the company if you don't mind."

"Not at all," she said.

Another knock at the door had me pausing. I sensed Missy peeking out of the kitchen as I went to answer it. Lucky stood protectively at my feet.

I opened the door to Quinn and Noah, and my heart sank. Fawn leaned toward Quinn, but I could see the seriousness of his expression and the unsure look on Noah's face. Something terrible was about to happen. I could feel it.

Quinn offered Fawn a smile and an adorable stuffed monkey with gigantic eyes, and she gingerly took it with a soft thank you. I knew she could sense the tension, and I turned to Missy, who rushed over with a smile and took Fawn from me.

"I'll take her to Roy's to get an ice cream, okay?" Missy's understanding tone brought strength to me. I nodded as the two hurried out the front door, past Quinn and Noah. I faced down two Lockharts. One I'd been dying to see and the other was his brother.

"What's going on?" I asked in a light voice, though I trembled inside. I knew what was going to happen. I didn't want to admit it to myself. They were going to fire me. The reason didn't matter. I'd lied about being fired, faked a letter of recommendation, caused problems at a worksite, and my ex had likely filed a pain and suffering suit against them for getting hurt at the job site. They had plenty of reasons to fire me, and I deserved to lose the job.

Why did the thought of being fired squeeze all the breath out of my lungs and leave me aching inside?

"Maybe we should sit down." Noah's calming voice appeared to smooth the tension from Quinn's shoulders as they seemed to lower a fraction of an inch.

"Sure." Putting on a brave face, I led them to the kitchen table, and we sat down. Lucky had stayed as close as he could without tripping me. The thought of what would happen next twisted my stomach in painful knots, but I was determined to put my best foot forward. "Would either of you like a drink? Coffee?" My gaze ticked to Quinn's without thinking about it, and I quickly glanced at Noah instead.

"No, thank you." Noah's slight head shake and Quinn's silence left me more nervous. I perched on the edge of my seat and waited. I thought about an old movie I'd seen with a prisoner walking toward the firing squad. I was facing the same thing, only a different kind of firing. I'd never identified with that scene more than I did at that moment, sitting with the brothers.

"Lauren, there's no easy way to do this, but you're fired." Quinn's words were resolute, and Noah's attention jerked to his brother and locked on him for what seemed like an eternity.

Time stood still as Noah demanded to talk to his brother. The two excused themselves for a moment to talk and headed for the front door as I sat numbly. What was I going to do now? Planting my elbows on the table, I put my head in my hands and tried to take deep breaths to calm my racing heart.

He fired me. Once again, I was out of work with little savings, no options, no job waiting, and nowhere to go. Maybe I'd have to call my parents and ask them for help, but I hated being a burden. Asking them to open their home to Fawn and me wouldn't be easy for anyone.

I'd failed. Mike was right when he'd spitefully told me I couldn't make it on my own the night I told him we were getting a divorce.

Stunned, I thought about Fawn, about uprooting our lives again, and my heart shattered. She'd be devastated. She liked it here, loved seeing her great grandparents, loved the town and the neighbor girl she'd made friends with.

How many times would I have to move her around? How many times would Mike thrust himself into our world and rip everything to shreds?

I sighed, staring at the dingy floor of the place we'd called home, watching Lucky slumber peacefully. I remembered Quinn saying the place had good bones, and I wondered if that had been his subtle offer to fix it up.

The door opened, and Lucky jerked awake as the men walked back in, their silent presence crushing my soul. They were the living embodiment of how I'd failed again. I lifted my head to watch them approach.

"Sorry about that," Quinn said.

Noah's furious expression told me precisely what he thought about his brother's action. Noah had always been in my corner. I couldn't help but wonder what he saw in me. His brother surely hadn't seen it in the beginning.

"No worries. I can sign an NDA about your business practices, and since I've only worked from home, I'll be out of your hair in no time." I offered Quinn a smile. "You said this place has good bones. I'll sell it to you for a steal of a deal?"

He didn't answer. Instead, he took a pink slip out of his pocket, placed it on the table, and slid it toward me. When his gaze met mine, the heat there stunned me, and my cheeks stung before I dropped my attention to the table. I didn't want to look at him or the pink slip or anything else.

Debt would swallow me whole if I couldn't get out from under this place. My prospects for getting another place without a job were slim. No matter how I looked at things, I knew I was in serious trouble.

This firing would ruin me.

"Well, thank you for everything," I said, struggling to stay gracious. "Working with Lockhart Construction was a pleasure."

There was nothing left to say.

"I have a proposal to make." Quinn's voice shifted, and I dared to meet his stare head-on. He didn't glance at Noah, who seemed to be confused and still angry.

"Okay, shoot." What could he possibly have in mind?

"I fired you for two reasons."

"I know. I lied and forged the letter of recommendation."

He chuckled, which seemed like an odd thing to do during a firing.

"Yes, you did, but that's not why. There's this issue of you and me and you working for me."

I cocked my head in confusion. "You're firing me because we have a thing?"

He nodded. "There's also the issue of full disclosure."

I wanted to sink into my chair. If only I'd been truthful.

"So, in order to rectify the problem, I'd like to rehire you again, but with a bonus." He pulled a mini pad of paper from his pocket, along with a pen, flipped it open, and wrote something down. He ripped the page out, folded it in half, then scooted it in my direction like he had the pink slip. This time, he didn't take his fingers off of it. Instead, he spoke directly to me.

"We don't care why you got fired. You're an asset to this company. We made a mistake hiring you on at the rate we did. You are worth so much more." He stared at Noah. "I usually handle hiring because these bozos have no idea what they're doing."

Noah rolled his eyes. And for a moment, they were boys again. I held back a grin at their antics as Quinn's attention returned to me. "We owe you a bonus for finding the previous skimming. That's already been figured out and will be deposited into your account within two to five business days."

I shook my head. "That was part of my job."

Quinn smiled. "You did it well and saved our credit scores as well as our reputations with several suppliers. Trust me, you earned the bonus, and it's not up for debate."

Noah nodded. "That would have cost us a lot of money down the road and would have cost relationships we couldn't have repaired. In this business, if you don't pay, you don't get suppliers or workers."

Warmth lit like a match in my heart, starting small and spreading outward.

"And that brings me to my second point," Quinn said, his eyes locking on mine. "Rehiring you." His intensity did funny things to my belly as he spoke up again. "I can't be your boss and your lover, so you will now be under Noah." He cleared his throat. "I mean you'll work for Noah and hopefully be under me." He gave me a silly, life-altering wink.

It was the deal of a lifetime.

"You've proven you're perfect for the job, and we'd be lost without you. What do you say?" His hopeful silence left me struggling to breathe. He *wanted* me back, and not just as an accountant.

I huffed. "Did you have to fire me?" I asked, the stress erupting from me. "Did you have to scare me like that?" I reached out and playfully smacked his shoulder. Then I hit it again as his features registered surprise and humor. Lucky woke up and yapped at Quinn, who seemed stunned and offered the little dog a treat.

"I thought you'd appreciate that I hired you based solely on your performance." His protests left Noah grinning as he pulled out of my reach. "I didn't want you to think that the past would or could ever be held over your head."

"I'd have trusted you if you just said that." I punctuated my words with another swat on his arm, and he pushed himself back.

"I didn't file the paperwork yet. I can shred it, and this whole conversation can be a secret between the three of us if you'd rather." I leaped to my feet, and Quinn took off.

I gave chase, the stress, fear, and anxiety all flowing out of me as I followed him down the hallway. Right behind me, Lucky slid on the floor, his barking ringing in my ears.

Quinn turned to face me, and I stopped in my tracks. His arms wound around my shoulders tightly. His warm gaze met mine, and he studied my eyes for a moment as the dog went quiet, clearly unsure of what to do.

"You're perfect," he murmured, his fingertip trailing along my cheek. "The past is done and gone. If you're ready to move forward, I'm right here by your side." His gentle words had that flame in me blazing into a roaring fire in no time, and I breathed a sigh of relief.

I stared at Quinn. "Don't you ever scare me like that again."

"Promise." Without hesitation, he lowered his lips to mine.

I'd wanted, more than anything, to forget my past and move forward, and Quinn would make that happen.

CHAPTER TWENTY-FOUR

QUINN

"Maybe I should go." Noah's voice reminded me he was in the room, and judging by the way Lauren jolted in my arms, she'd forgotten about him, too.

My plan had worked. Maybe it hadn't worked how I hoped, but it worked. Lauren didn't have to worry about the past coming back to haunt her. She knew she was working with us because she was perfect for the job, and now there was one thing left I had to tell her. I'd wait until my brother left, though.

"See you. Thanks for the backup," I said as he walked past. I had him come with me to make sure that I had another person there to help if anything went wrong.

With a knowing smile, he told us both goodbye and left the house. Lucky stared after him, then looked up at us as if unsure we noticed the stranger had gone.

"I'm sorry for scaring you. I swear I didn't intend for that to happen." I stroked her hair back from her face. "I just wanted you to know that no matter what else, you'd *earned* your place with us."

She nodded, her arms slipping around my back. "I know. I

finally feel like I belong here, and that's amazing. You could've been nicer about it, though."

I chuckled. "I didn't consider how this could've backfired on me, and I should have." Giving her a gentle squeeze, I let her go and led her toward the couch. We sat side by side as Lucky popped up to sit between us. "What are you going to do next?" I asked, glancing at her as I petted Lucky. He rolled to his back and offered me his belly as the end of his stubby tail flapped quickly.

Lauren stared off into space. "I think I'd like to fix this place up." She gestured to the house, and I nodded, thinking about how I could help her. "I'd also like to see my grandparents more often since they live so close." She trailed off, nibbling her lip. "This isn't what you meant by asking what I would do next."

I smiled that she'd caught on.

"Oh. You mean about Mike, don't you?" Her face scrunched up, and the urge to kiss her nearly overwhelmed me. "I've already talked to my parents about being go-betweens. I'm cutting contact with him." I expected her to waiver, but she continued strongly. "I'm going to start over without him in my life at all."

Pride swelled up in me. "Let me know how I can help." I'd do anything to protect her and Fawn.

With a smile, she stood up and offered me her hand. When I took it, she tugged me to my feet and led me to Fawn's room.

Inside, on Fawn's dresser, an army of little toys watched from the closet while the solar system sat on her white desk. The entire room had that pretty, child-like femininity to it, and the toys I'd been giving her fit right in.

"They're her favorite." She motioned to the toys that nearly filled the dresser top. "She says they keep her safe. It's the cutest thing ever. She likes you, and that's kind of scary and sweet all at once."

My heart filled with wonder that such a small thing, some cute plushy toys I'd been collecting for her, meant so much to her.

"And she loves this." Lauren walked over to set the planets in motion around the sun, and I grinned.

"It brings back wonderful memories." I remembered how I'd spend hours thinking about the vastness of space and how spectacularly small we were considering the size of the solar system. And how much smaller we seemed when thinking about the galaxy and beyond. Somehow, that always helped me put my issues in perspective. I think that was my father's reason for giving me that toy.

"And she's making wonderful memories with it, I think." As she walked back to me, Lauren's smile told me a story of love, trust, and joy. "I owe you an apology. I am sorry for lying to you."

"I forgive you." Life is too short to hold grudges.

Her expression darkened. "And about what Mike said ... the reason he gave that I'd been fired."

I shook my head. "None of my business. If it's true, if it's false, I don't care." What she did before she met me wasn't any of my concern.

"Really?" She seemed stunned.

"Really. What you did before we met isn't my business. True or not, I don't care, and it doesn't change my opinion of you if that's a concern." Her concern that her past mattered to me was endearing and heartbreaking. That she cared what I thought about her told me everything I needed to know about how she felt about me.

"Well, it's not true. He made it up. I didn't sleep with anyone at my previous job. He got me fired because of his inappropriate behavior." Her fists balled up at her sides, and I could see fury rolling off her and sending tremors through her frame.

"I'm sorry he did that to you." She deserved better than that. I hoped she'd figured that out, too.

My words seemed to drain the fight out of her, and a slight smile crossed her lips. She moved toward the door, and we ducked out of Fawn's room and headed back toward the living room.

"I had another question for you," I said.

She glanced at me, a curious crease on her forehead. "Sure, ask away."

My palms were sweating, and a nervous ringing in my ears bothered me, but I pushed forward as we sat back down on the couch next to the sleeping Lucky. He woke up and looked from me to her before putting his head back down. His eye blinked, and his lid drooped lower and lower as his breathing deepened again and he drifted off to sleep.

"I was wondering if you'd be interested in dating." I realized this might have confused her, so I clarified. "Me."

Her smile lit up her face as she studied me. "Isn't that why you put Noah as my boss? No more conflict of interest?"

"Yes, but I should've asked if that's what you want. Do you want me?"

"You're a hard sell, Quinn Lockhart, but you have good bones and I think there's hope for you yet." A laugh escaped her, and I couldn't stop staring. She was beautiful, and I wanted, more than anything, to kiss her.

I pulled her close and leaned in.

The door opened, and we jerked apart. Missy walked in with Fawn asleep in her arms. She watched us curiously. "She had ice cream, then started dozing. Did I give you enough time?"

"You did, thank you." I nodded at her, but she seemed more focused on Lauren than me.

"Everything is fine. Thank you for taking her out. Did she have fun?" Lauren walked over and took the sleeping child from her friend. Fawn woke up as Lucky came trotting over, looking up at his tiny human in her mother's arms.

"I had chocolate," Fawn said before going back to sleep.

I walked over and lifted her in my arms. "I'll put her to bed if you'd like to talk to your friend." The two of them had things to discuss.

Lauren relinquished her daughter after a second's hesitation, and I carried her to her bedroom and laid her on her bed. Pulling the pale-pink blankets up over her, I picked up a book and kneeled at the side of her bed to read in a soft voice.

As I told the tale of a princess who saved herself and befriended a dragon, I enjoyed the quiet moment, thinking about my parents. They'd read to me as a child. Even being one of four boys, they'd always made time for each of us. I always felt loved, cared for, and protected. As every child should, I believed.

Lauren would do a fantastic job protecting her daughter, and I'd be there as backup when she needed me. I'd keep bringing Fawn little trinkets, toys, and other fun things, and I'd make sure she knew how important she was and how much she meant to the people in her life.

As the story drew to a close, I watched her sleep for a moment. She looked like her mother with those long lashes, and I wondered if I'd ever have kids of my own.

I relished the thought of passing down my father's love and wisdom. The possibility of instilling love and joy into a little human being made me happy.

"He's making my ovaries tingle. If you don't snatch him up, I will." Missy's voice carried into the room. With a smile, I put the book back on the shelf and left Fawn's room to join the adults.

"He's going to hear you," Lauren said as I stepped quietly out of Fawn's room. Missy saw me right away, but Lauren's back was to me.

"Are you saying he doesn't make your ovaries tingle? Girl, you better get him on lockdown, or I'm going to chase him." Missy licked her lips, her playful expression only betrayed by the sparkle in her eyes.

"He does, and I think I'm in love with him already."

Missy's satisfied smile as she winked at me didn't hit me nearly as hard as Lauren's confession.

"He's right behind me, isn't he?" Lauren's mortified voice

brought a grin to my face, and I stood there as she turned around, her expression horrified.

"I heard every word," I said.

"So did we. Great bedtime story you picked," Missy said, studying me. "How'd you know it's the house favorite?"

I lifted both shoulders. "Just picked one at random. Lucky, I guess." At his name, the dog perked up, wagged his tail, and hopped off the couch to trot in my direction.

"I hear you're good to her," Missy said. "But what she says doesn't matter. I can tell she's happy. Try to keep her happy, because she deserves it." She made a face at Lauren, who tried to blow off her words.

"I agree." I walked up to stand behind Lauren and stroked the tension out of her shoulders. As she relaxed, I made myself a promise to always be on her side. To fight beside her, to be her friend, her partner. If sides were ever picked, I'd choose hers, no matter what.

I wanted to be sure she had an easier go of life. She had it hard, and I was done letting her struggle.

"Well, I guess that's that, then." Missy shrugged. "I'll start planning the wedding—"

"No! We're taking it slow," Lauren said, and I chuckled as Missy pursed her lips and wiggled them side to side, clearly not believing her friend.

"Right." Missy glanced at me. "So summer, you think?"

I shook my head. "I'm not about to plan a wedding without her permission." With a smile at Lauren, I continued talking. "Of course, I'm going to do everything in my power to be the next man she wants to marry. I hope that's enough for you, Missy."

Missy stood up and pointed an aggressive index finger at me. "I'm going to hold you to that."

I had a feeling she absolutely would.

EPILOGUE
LAUREN

Three months later...

I sat at the table with Quinn on one side. On the other, my mother and my father sat side by side. They were holding hands and smiling at one another with all the love in the world silently communicated between them. And at the head of the table, Quinn's mom, Irene, seemed to survey her kingdom.

We'd joined the family dinner along with my grandparents, Ethel and Norman. Fawn played with one of her stuffed unicorns at the kids' table and talked to little Kip, who sat in his highchair. She offered the unicorn to Kip, who took it and promptly shoved it in his mouth. Laughter from Kandra as she took the toy, thanked Fawn, and gave it back, warmed my heart.

We felt like a family.

Mike had never introduced me to his father. I always thought it was because I wouldn't live up to his standards. Now I was sure it had more to do with how disappointing his father found him.

Quinn's arm slipped around my shoulders as he told his mother about how the paperwork was done, and we were free. Of course, Irene knew we were talking about my ex-husband. Mike had walked out of my life the second I proved I was through with him. It took refusing to answer fifty-three calls, calling Miranda when he just showed up at my house several times without permission, and my parents taking Fawn to his home for his visitation.

He wanted nothing to do with us unless he could get to me, and that was fine. My only concern was for Fawn, but she'd taken the news a lot better than I expected.

She'd nearly given me a heart attack when she asked if Quinn would be her father now. I remembered the moment perfectly in my mind, and I melted a little, thinking about it.

Quinn had kneeled beside her and asked her what she wanted. Fawn responded in her tiniest voice that she liked Quinn and wanted him to be her dad. They hugged, and I had held back tears.

Mike had been mad to find out that he had no grounds to sue the Lockhart brothers after his "fall." I think he'd been more upset over that than giving up his daughter. Given how many people were there and heard him being told he couldn't be on the job site, the judge seemed ready to press trespassing charges should the brothers wish to do so, but they declined.

I'd also been informed I could push a defamation lawsuit, but I wanted to be done with my ex. When I gave up, the weight of the world lifted off my shoulders, and I could breathe easily for the first time in as long as I could remember. I hadn't realized how much he'd been dragging me down.

I watched Fawn play happily as Quinn gently nudged me. Glancing at him, I noticed he was facing Irene, and I glanced at her, confused. The slight smile on her face told me I'd missed something.

"I'm sorry, I was miles away." I smiled and shifted in my seat as Quinn's hand came to rest on my knee.

"I wanted to make sure Quinn's treating you well." Irene's soft voice left Quinn's back straightening, and I didn't doubt he was on pins and needles, waiting for my response.

"He's amazing." I took his hand and smiled at him as he took a bite of the delicious homemade mac and cheese my mother had brought as her contribution to dinner.

The soft chatter around the table left me feeling warm and loved. Ethan and Angie were smiling at one another, quiet and in love. Bayden and Miranda were having a conversation, and Kandra was on one side of Kip with Noah on the other. Both of them were talking to and loving on Fawn, who basked in their attention.

"I'm happy, to be honest." I smiled at Irene, and my parents gave each other private grins and leaned in close, clearly pleased with the news.

"That's good." Irene's eyes crinkled at the corners as she scanned the table and looked at all her children, grandchildren, and their loves. I could see the joy in her eyes and knew that she was happy with the life she'd built around herself. For a moment, I hoped I'd be half as lucky as her when my child was grown. I could only hope Fawn would want to spend as much time with me as Irene's kids wanted to spend with her.

Then again, I enjoyed my time with my parents, too. Maybe that would be normal to her.

"What she's leaving out," Quinn said after swallowing his bite of food. "Is that she's the amazing one. She's saved us money, renegotiated deals for us, and has been keeping the books meticulously. Every dime is accounted for, and there hasn't been a missed or late payment since she took us on." Quinn squeezed my knee under the table as my heart swelled.

"Oh, stop. I'm just doing my job." My cheeks burned.

"She's already fixed my credit score after that last fiasco. So don't you believe her for a second." Noah's voice rose above, and Kandra nodded.

"It's a big deal to us." Kandra's soft voice exuded her thanks, and I lowered my head to stare at the food on my plate. I'd never felt as appreciated or important as I felt here with the Lockhart family. No other job treated me as well, and no other coworkers were as good of friends.

"Thank you. I'm just happy to be here. It could've gone so differently." I gave Quinn a side-eye, reminding him of how he'd fired me. His reckless move could've resulted in so much stress and headache, but he'd shredded the firing paperwork, and it was as if it had never happened. Only Noah, Quinn, and I knew the whole story, but that fresh start still meant the world to me.

He lifted his brow in an innocent expression, a mouthful of mac and cheese puffing his cheeks out slightly. I couldn't help but laugh. Under the table, Lucky shifted and got up. I peeked and watched him walk over to Fawn. He curled up under her feet, yawned, and promptly went back to sleep.

I couldn't believe how fortunate I was. Quinn was the man for me.

I loved him more than I ever thought possible. Maybe I'd been falling in love with him all along. The last few months, though, had deepened our feelings. When he held me, I could imagine forever in his arms.

We had fun together. We'd taken Fawn to the aquarium, the zoo, and the planetarium. No matter how long the drive, Quinn helped me pack and made sure she had enough snacks. He set fun playlists for her to sing to in the car, and we enjoyed each other's company.

Now, as the warm, inviting room pressed close, voices buzzed, and the picture of Quinn's father looked down at us from the head of the table beside Irene, I basked in the love. Quinn leaned into me as he told my parents and his mother about the trips we'd taken and how much Fawn loved the seals and how she'd gasped when the planetarium went dark, and the stars lit up the ceiling.

"I remember when your father took you, Quinn." Irene's smile told me she knew as well as I did that Quinn was passing all his father's love to Fawn.

Quinn nodded. "Me too."

He bought her books about stars and a telescope, and most nights, I'd catch them looking up at the stars. By day, we fixed up my house, turning it into a home together. Everything we did, no matter how small, was done with love.

"Look at him, Mom," Fawn said, drawing my attention to Kip as he wiggled happily in his chair while grinning at her. She wiggled back, an enormous smile on her face. Watching them play sent a collective *aww* through the room, and Kandra took a video while Noah made faces at Fawn until she laughed and almost fell over.

Everything was right in the world, and I couldn't imagine being happier as I took a bite of potato salad that melted in my mouth. Yep, these family dinners would make me fat in no time. Somehow, I didn't think Quinn would like me any less. He loved me wholeheartedly, and as with everything he did, he threw all of himself into it and did nothing in halves. He might be reckless, but he was mine, and I planned to keep him forever if he wanted to stay.

"Are you okay?" he asked in a low voice. I realized tears were welling up as I thought about how impossibly perfect my life was. I thought after Mike I'd wind up alone. Heck, I'd wanted to be alone because of my ex. Now I'd found love and joy and I wouldn't trade this for anything.

"Yes, I'm better than okay," I whispered back as his fingers threaded with mine under the table. "I've never been happier."

He lit up with my words and leaned in to plant a kiss on my cheek. The promise in that gentle touch stunned me. No words could've better explained the depth of his feelings for me. I was absolutely in love with him.

I glanced around, remembering a similar dinner with the Lockharts when I sat in the same chair and met the family, only this time, everything went differently. Last time, I believed Quinn hated me. Today, I knew he loved me.

A SNEAK PEEK AT ONE HUNDRED REASONS

There were three things Sage Nichols knew with absolute certainty:

Death couldn't be escaped.

Mr. Right Now was never Mr. Right.

Hell wasn't fire and brimstone; it was a cold April day in Denver.

In the dark, dank basement of her sister's house, Sage held up two sets of scrubs and looked at her dog, Otis, who was sprawled across the bed. This was the time of night his poor body gave out. Missing a hind leg took a lot out of the golden retriever.

He lifted his head, and his amber eyes looked between the two uniforms. He touched the blue one with his wet snout.

"Blue it is."

She ruffled the fur around his neck, and Otis rolled to his back while she gave him his final belly rub of the night. He pulled back his lips to show his teeth in what she could only describe as a smile.

If Sage didn't hurry, she'd be late to work. She yanked at her unruly curls and forced them into hair tie submission. Dressed, she took the stairs two at a time up to the main level. The exertion got her blood pumping so she'd be ready to take on the triple-shot latte her sister Lydia would pass off at the front door. After two years of working the night shift at the hospital, Sage should be used to the schedule, but she needed that surge of adrenaline that came from three hundred milligrams of caffeine.

Keys jingled in the front door lock, and Sage greeted her sister with a "Hey, Doc. How was your day?"

Lydia handed over the coffee. "Too long. One gunshot wound. One car accident. Can you believe a little boy broke his arm and leg playing Superman? He tied a tablecloth around his neck like it was a cape and jumped off the roof." Lydia shook her head and wrapped Sage in a bear hug and squeezed. "Have a good night. Don't kill anyone."

"That's always the goal." Sage laughed at their conversation. Anyone unaware that Lydia was an ER doctor at Denver General and Sage was a nurse in the geriatric ward of the same hospital might find the comment shocking. Sadly, despite the gang fights, shootings, and car accidents average for the city, Sage saw more death than her sister.

The door closed behind Sage, and she walked into the thick layer of fog, normal for the spring when winter battled for its final breath. It was as if the cold had wrapped its fingers around the city and refused to let go.

She hopped into her RAV4, started the engine, and pulled out of the driveway to cut through the arctic chill one mile at a time. Normally, the trip to work took twenty minutes, but with poor visibility, she'd be lucky to make it in thirty. She sipped her latte. At least she'd have enough time to wake up before she had to make her rounds and fill out patient charts.

On the seat beside her was a stack of pink paper and envelopes for her favorite patient, Bea Bennett, the third such delivery in as many weeks. It was a good trade. She supplied paper, and Bea brought sunshine into Sage's otherwise gloomy life. Hospitalized for pericarditis, Bea spent her days writing letters that seemed to disappear as quickly as Sage brought supplies.

Fluorescent lighting blinded her as she pulled into the parking spot reserved for the night-shift employees. There was no name on a placard for her. That benefit was reserved for important people like Lydia's boyfriend, Dr. Adam McKay, the hottie who ran the ER.

"Everyone make it through the day?" Sage asked her colleague Tina as she arrived on the ninth-floor ward. She tucked her purse into the desk drawer and set the stationery down on the desk for a later delivery. Tina handed over the clipboard so she could leave. The halls of the ward were quiet except for the beeping of heart monitors and the whir of oxygen tanks. All seemed in order.

Tina tucked the hair that had fallen from her ponytail behind her ears. "It's been a busy day."

That wasn't the answer Sage wanted, but it was typical because talking about patients would keep Tina there a few more minutes, and she gave no one extra time. Five minutes later, Sage started her rounds, checking vitals and stats as she moved down the hallway of the nearly full ward. She pulled a chart from a once-empty room to find it was now occupied with a new patient. "Clive Russell." Saying the name out loud helped reinforce the fact that these were real, living, breathing people, not just medical notes and numbers on a page.

Sage skimmed through his records and understood that Clive's life clock wouldn't be ticking much longer. He had stage four pancreatic cancer. A shiver raced down her spine. Of all the cancers she'd seen eat up her patients, pancreatic cancer seemed to be the one with the sharpest teeth and biggest appetite. It weighed on her that she couldn't save these people. She cared for them and did her best to bring them joy in their final days, but it wasn't enough.

She pasted on a brilliant smile and walked into his room.

Monitors beeped, and the air was filled with a scent that seemed to be synonymous with the elderly. Sage tried to figure the smell out, but the closest thing she could ever come up with was Bengay for arthritis mixed with contraband candy.

At ten o'clock at night, her patients were often fast asleep, but not this one. He was sitting up in bed with his thick gray mane of hair shooting in every direction, a roadmap of lines etched deep into his smiling face. At eighty years old, he still had all his teeth, which surprised her. His hand gripped the remote control. The glow of the television lit up his jaundiced skin.

"Hello, Mr. Russell," Sage said in a quick, caffeine-induced rush.

"I told them not to send in my date until after the news." His eyes shifted between her and the television.

While he watched his show, Sage moved through her checklist, which started with vitals and ended with fluids.

She wrapped his arm with the blood pressure cuff and pumped the inflation bulb. The bladder filled and released as she counted the ebb and flow to his arteries. "I couldn't wait to see you," Sage said as she swiped the thermometer across his forehead and recorded his numbers. "They told me there was a handsome new man in town, but they didn't do you justice." She checked his IV fluid levels and the output from the bag collecting his urine.

The old man grinned. "Call me Clive. I mean, since we're on our first date and all." His blue eyes shone behind the veil of ill health.

"You're a charmer, I see. Just the way I like my men—with a bit of mischief and a lot of sweet." The fact that Clive Russell, a man fifty years her senior, was as close to being her boyfriend as any living, breathing person with a Y chromosome spoke to the sad state of her love life.

"A beauty like you must have a boyfriend." He adjusted his pillow and flopped back.

"Oh, I do. His name is Otis, and he has a thing for kibble and Milk-Bones."

Clive laughed, then winced.

She filled his water and pulled a spare blanket from the

cupboard in case he got chilled during the night. "Well, Clive, every-thing looks great." *Great* being a relative term, its scale ran the gamut from "great for almost dead" to "great, you'll make it out of here alive." Clive ranked closer to the former. Even though the pallor of impending death dulled his skin, she was buoyed because Clive clutched on to every moment of life he had left. Or at least he gripped the remote control as if it contained magic elixir, and to Clive, it might because he was not watching the news like he said. No, Clive was watching *Game of Thrones*, which included a weekly naked dose of a blonde beauty called Khaleesi.

"Let me know when you get to the weather report." Sage patted the old man's hand.

She left him to his "news" with a promise to check in on him later, then continued her patient rounds. Mr. Dumont needed pain meds. Mrs. Young, who had celebrated her ninety-first birthday yesterday, needed a new IV bag. Nora Croxley needed a hug. Mr. Nolan needed to be slapped upside the head for flashing his old man parts for the second time this week.

In her second-favorite patient's room, Sage found him sneaking a Snickers bar. "No junk food for you." She confiscated the candy and reminded David Lark that a man with diabetes shouldn't feed his disease.

"Come on! I gave up women. I gave up alcohol. I gave up swear-ing. I'm dying." He watched her tuck the candy bar into her pocket.

"Not on my shift." There was no dying allowed on Sage's shift. That was one of her silly rules. One she could never enforce. She understood dying was a part of life. The minute a human was born, they started to die, but somewhere deep inside, she believed if she cared enough, worked hard enough, and brought joy to those around her, it would be enough to keep them tethered to this world.

As Sage passed the nurses' station, she picked up the packet of pink stationery from the desk. She shouldn't have favorites, but she did. Bea was hers. Just walking into the older woman's room lifted

Sage's spirits. Despite Bea's failing health, she was full of life. It didn't hurt that she also reminded Sage of Grandma Nichols—"Grandma Dotty"—with her head of white hair and a voice sweeter than honey.

Her mind skated around distant memories of her grandma who had stepped up to love and care for her and Lydia when their parents died. Had they really been gone for fifteen years? Grandma Dotty for two? She couldn't believe how quickly time evaporated.

Sage stopped at the lounge to get two cups of coffee—sweet and creamy for Bea, black and bitter for herself. She tucked the writing paper under her arm and hurried toward Bea's room, ready for a hug and another story.

Bea entertained her with tales about her hometown of Aspen Cove. A town straight out of a television series. A place where everyone had enough. No one went without. All residents, though not related, were considered kin. Sage knew the stories were told from the perspective of a woman looking back on her life, where the memory was sweeter than the reality, but Bea told it all in a way that made it sound possible.

Coffee in hand, Sage turned her back on the closed door, pressed the handle down with her elbow, and shoved her tail end into the room. It was alarmingly silent and almost black, except for the outline of an empty bed. Bea was gone. The pink stationary fell from her arm and hit the floor, spreading out like a carpet to soak up the coffee that fell next. Sage stumbled back to the wall and slid down to the cold industrial floor—the lifeless white tile that filled the hallways of so many institutions. As the pink stationery soaked up the spilled coffee, Sage came to terms with the reality that Bea was gone.

There was no way she'd been released. Just yesterday she'd had a cardiac MRI, and no changes were noted in her condition. Nothing was better, but nothing was worse. Pericarditis didn't cure itself overnight. No, her Bea had passed, and with her went one of the final sparks of light that shone in Sage's eyes.

Sage pulled herself into a tight little ball and buried her face against her knees. She released a wail that sounded foreign but vibrated deep within her soul. She knew she needed to get on her feet and resume her shift, but her arms wouldn't move from the hug in which she wrapped herself. Her eyes remained shut, trying to stanch the coming flood of tears. Her heart beat with a sluggish rhythm that negated the effects of her latte.

Why did Bea's life mean so much more than the others? Why did her death create a cavernous hole inside her? It was one more loss in a life full of them. One more soul she'd tried to hold on to without success. Another person who abandoned her before she could say goodbye.

GET A FREE BOOK.

Go to www.authorkellycollins.com

ABOUT THE AUTHOR

International bestselling author of more than thirty novels, Kelly Collins writes with the intention of keeping love alive. Always a romantic, she blends real-life events with her vivid imagination to create characters and stories that lovers of contemporary romance, new adult, and romantic suspense will return to again and again.

For More Information
www.authorkellycollins.com
kelly@authorkellycollins.com

ALSO BY BY KELLY COLLINS

An Aspen Cove Romance Series

One Hundred Reasons

One Hundred Heartbeats

One Hundred Wishes

One Hundred Promises

One Hundred Excuses

One Hundred Christmas Kisses

One Hundred Lifetimes

One Hundred Ways

One Hundred Goodbyes

One Hundred Secrets

One Hundred Regrets

One Hundred Choices

One Hundred Decisions

One Hundred Glances

One Hundred Lessons

One Hundred Mistakes

One Hundred Nights

One Hundred Whispers

One Hundred Reflections

One Hundred Intentions

Cross Creek Novels